DRAGONS' MATE

HER ROYAL DRAGON PACK BOOK 3

ALEX LIDELL

CHAPTER 1

Kit

Quinton shoves me into a shadowed corner. I land hard on the wooden floor, my body ringing at the sudden impact. My quilt falls from my grip, leaving me naked. Twisting around, I see Quinton on his knees, blood welling up around the arrow shaft that now protrudes from the dragon prince's chest. The arrow that had been meant for me. A shiver runs through me, one that has nothing to do with cold.

Breathing in a lungful of dust, I watch as Quinton grabs the shaft and yanks it out of his flesh in a quick motion that makes me blanche. In the sliver of light coming through the open window, I see blood dripping from the wound and staining his shirt.

"Stay here and stay down," Quinton orders. Moving faster than anyone should be able to—much less someone who has just been shot—he streaks toward the window and goes through it in a fluid motion. We are on the second floor and I try not to think about the jump down. Not that I'm dumb enough to go look. No one knew Quinton was in my chambers, so I know I'd been the archer's intended target.

I don't know why. I'm no one. A human slave taken for a dragon's hoard and then sent away by the Massa'eve king. I'm irrelevant. At least I was until the world turned on its head in the past hour and tied me forever to a dragon prince.

Heart pounding, I stay where I am in the shadowed corner, not even daring to pull the quilt toward me. Seconds tick away, turning to minutes, and my thoughts start to order themselves. As good as darkness is for concealment, it won't do much if someone decides to lob another arrow through the open window. Even a blind shot would land *somewhere*. A bit of shielding would not be amiss just now.

Pulling myself together, I crawl from the corner to the space beneath the bed. It's stuffy and even dustier than the bare floor was—but it would protect me from any more arrows at least. I'd not thought twice about having left the window open earlier in the evening. Would things have turned out differently if I took care?

Pillowing my head in my arms, I curl up as much as the space under the bed allows. I hate being helpless, unable to do anything but hide under a dusty bed. But I'm a human in the realm of immortal fae, dragon princes and ancient magics. It isn't exactly a fair playing field.

And yet I'd just signed myself up to wade right into the middle of that immortal mess. Suddenly, the notions of sneaking back to the palace, infiltrating the pledge ball, and getting myself accepted into the Equinox Trials all seem like very bad life choices. Especially since attaining the precious dose of the fertility elixir, which is the trials' prize, will mean some poor human becoming the pack's brood mare.

The bite on my breast tingles, the new bond between Quinton and me reminding me of its existence. Because on top of everything else, a dragon prince had accidently lost control and claimed me as his mate less than an hour ago. A dragon prince who I don't even like, and who likes me even less. Neither of those things are likely to change. Quinton dislikes weakness—and being human in the immortal realm is about as weak as it gets. Worse, being shackled to me makes Quinton weaker. My very existence is a vulnerability to him.

Which he will never let me forget.

The tingling sensation around my breast intensifies, like icy-hot tendrils curling around the mark. I've no idea where Quinton is or what he is doing exactly, but it's something intense. Intense good or intense bad, though? And according to what measure? Dismembering someone would probably be *good* in Quinton's book, so I couldn't trust the bond to be objective even if it were more obliging with information.

At least I know Quinton is alive.

I'm not sure how much time passes before there is a muffled thump in the room and soft footsteps approaching my hiding spot. I know it's Quinton even before he lifts the bed from above me and shoves it aside as if it weighs no more than a heavy chair.

In the band of moonlight coming through the window, Quinton's preternaturally beautiful features are taut with displeasure. His broad shoulders and chest heave with heavy breaths, his blood soaked tunic clinging to his skin. The scent of blood coming off him is so intense that I want to recoil. But then Quinton's silver eyes catch mine and everything inside me twists into a knot. No part of me wants to go near the dragon right now, and yet every part of me needs to. Not just near... My body longs for something a great deal deeper than *near.*

Remembering that I'm still curled up naked on the floor, I scramble up and grab the fallen quilt, pulling it around myself. "The blood," I say, fighting down my body's unwelcome reaction. "Are you alright?"

Quinton doesn't move, but the way his whole attention zeros in on me feels like a physical act. His fevered gaze scans me from head to toe, his hands opening and closing at his sides. The singular focus is at once intimate and disconcerting.

I swallow. Now that we are close, the need to feel his body inside mine is washing over me in a heated blaze that is more than inappropriate.

"Quinton," I repeat. "The blood. Are you—"

"It's not mine," he says roughly. "Not most of it, anyway."
He looks down at himself as if seeing the mess for the first
time. Gripping the hem of the soaked shirt, the prince strips
it off, the material falling to the floor in a wet plop. "Better?"

That's a loaded question right now. Glad as I am that he is no
longer standing in blood-drenched clothes, I wish he had
something else to put on because damn it—I can't think over
the pounding primal desire suddenly seizing my chest and
my sex and everything in-between.

The run of Quinton's silver scales traces an intricate
pattern over smooth skin and chiseled muscles. One
column of scales, the one running down his sternum,
through the groove of his six-pack abs and down into the
flaps of his leather britches, makes it near impossible to
focus on anything but desire commandeering my senses.
The scales shimmer in whatever scraps of light they can
find.

My sex pulses. My breaths quicken. My mind fights for
clarity with every fiber of its being. "What... what happened?"
I ask him. The wound on his chest, which I finally find, is
raw but not nearly as bad as it would be on a human.

"Yirel and Jared. Your guards. Got drunk. Got stupid. Got
dead." Quinton runs his hand through his hair. The blond
strands are hanging loose and brushing his shoulder. He
pants as he speaks, though I don't think it's entirely from the
fight. Whatever is happening to me, is happening to him too.
"They wanted to end their assignment early. They got their
wish."

My guards. The ones who I'd started to believe were no one to be concerned over.

"Are you sure?" I ask, trying to clear my head. "You don't think Salazar or Geoffrey found out about me and -"

"I'm certain." A muscle ticks along Quinton's jaw and I suddenly notice that there is blood on his boots as well. Quinton raises his chin, and I catch a flash of icy harness flicker across his features. "We had a chat. They acted alone."

Oh stars. Did he...

"Yes. I did," Quinton says to the question I never spoke aloud but one that must have been evident in my eyes. There is no apology or even regret on his face. "Plus, if my uncle or cousin were behind this, they'd do better than lob blind arrows. As it was, the drunk buffoons' arrows barely had enough force to wound a human."

Quinton would know. Because he is the king's trained assassin. A killer. The one dragon prince who hates himself so much that he does everything he can to bring all the darkness in the world atop himself. I want to shove him into a wall for the brutality that he carries like a badge of honor. But I want his cock inside me more.

Stars take me. I'm so hot now that, despite the chill, a bead of sweat is rolling down my temple and the need blazing low in my belly is so fierce that it hurts. I clutch my quilt, too aware of the moisture slipping along my thighs as my head grows more hazy with each passing heartbeat. I focus on Quinton's pulsing bulge, unable to even look anywhere else.

"What's happening to me?" My voice cracks with the question. I force my glare up to Quinton's face, warning him to not even try feigning misunderstanding. Dragons smell arousal. He knows I'm wet. Just as he knows that I don't want to want him. "What did you do?"

"I bit you," Quinton says.

The bite on my breast flares. It seems to like being mentioned and acknowledged.

"This pull you feel is a side effect." Quinton draws in a deep breath, the flaps of his britches straining beneath the force of the growing bulge. Cursing, he backs a step away from me—only to bump against the dresser. "It's temporary. It will pass."

"When?"

He winces. "I don't know."

"Seriously?"

"I... I'm sorry."

"Sorry? You are rutting sorry?" Fury flashes through me. I didn't sign up for this. Didn't ask for my body to ignore my wishes while need so fierce that it hurts spills into my blood. Quinton did this. It's his bloody fault. My hand curls into a fist and I launch myself at him, swinging into his jaw. The quilt I'd been clutching flutters to the floor.

Quinton lets me connect, but the impact hurts my hand more than it hurts him. My anger roars. I punch again, but this time Quinton grabs my wrist and spins me into the wall like a ragdoll.

I put out my hand, barely saving my face from connecting with the plaster. *Asshole*.

My heart hammers. I yank my wrist from Quinton's grip. It works. I don't know—or care—whether he released me or if this madness has given me a surge of some preternatural strength. My vision frays at the edges. I shove away from the wall and kick Quinton's knee, the way the bastard himself taught me.

Quinton twists and takes the blow on his thigh, a snarl coming from deep inside his chest. His eyes swim with magic, the pupils more elongated than normal.

I shove his chest, aiming for his wound.

My palm barely touches him before he's moved out of the way, but a roar that might be pain or fury or something else entirely echoes through the small room. The next thing I know, Quinton slams my back into the wall so hard that bits of flaked plaster and paint rain down on us both. Then his body is pressing into me, his bulging cock digging into my stomach.

I yank the laces on the front of his britches, freeing him.

Quinton's shaft springs free. It's large and velvety, with the columns of scales along it glistening with moisture and fat drops clinging to the tip.

My mouth waters. I remember exactly how he tastes. I try to move, but he holds me flush against the wall.

"You are a rutting asshole," I shout at him. I'm not sure if I'm more mad that he has me pinned or that he is taking so damn long.

Whatever it is, Quinton absorbs it all. His nostrils flare. Then he is grabbing my hips and lifting me until I'm in line with his pulsating shaft.

I wrap my hands around his shoulders and he sheathes himself inside me in a single hard stroke. There is an instant of pain as the great size of him stretches everything inside me, but then he pumps and the thick head of his cock finds all the erotically sensitive points inside my channel. He runs over them as if playing piano keys.

Primal pleasure so intense it makes me dizzy rolls through me. I don't know where my body ends and the pulsing magic of our mating bond begins. Quinton pulls back and thrusts. Again. Again. Each of his strokes bangs me against the hard plaster. There is nothing kind or seductive about this taking. No, it's brutal and punishing.

And it's exactly what I crave.

CHAPTER 2

Quinton

Quinton roared as Kit's nails raked along his biceps, leaving tracks of erotic heat in their wake. Her usually warm chocolate eyes flared, sparks of magic mixing with the violent, primal pleasure filling them. Quinton's entire body pulsed with need as he thrust into her, each *stroke, stroke, stroke* of his cock in her channel echoing in his bones. His soul. It was all one cadence. The thrusts, the hearts pounding in both their chests, the bond that pulsated between them.

Power flooded Quinton's blood, as carnal and wild as

anything he'd ever felt. And not just him. He felt the magic flow through the bond into the human's veins, feeding her body with the strength and power needed to answer the mating's frenzied demand. Flakes of plaster from the aged wall rained down on Kit's head, an erratic symphony of groans from the old wooden floorboards harmonizing with the rutting they now hosted.

Kit threw back her head, exposing her neck to him. The implicit trust of the gesture nearly ended it for him. Quinton roared again as he gripped Kit tighter, driving himself in with each pounding stroke. Kit's wide pupils were glazing with her coming release and the spiking scent of Kit's arousal filled the space between them. It was a heady sweet aroma that overpowered the room's dank musk and it flared more each time Quinton entered Kit's channel, only to howl with frustration whenever he pulled back. Like a tug of war.

Feeling Kit's channel clamp around him, Quinton gripped her hips tighter, adding extra support to the thighs she'd wrapped around his waist. Kit undulated with every thrust of his hips, her whimpering betraying how close to release she was coming. The pressure inside Quinton rose with each heartbeat. His thrusts intensified mercilessly until he was pounding so hard that Kit jolted with each assault. Again. Again. The wet sound of their connection mixed with their breaths.

Kit opened her mouth, a primal moan escaping her throat.

Quinton gritted his teeth and pulled back. Held.

"Asshole," Kit growled.

Quinton bared his canines.

Kit bit him.

Quinton jerked as her teeth sank into the tender spot on his neck, right over his pulse. The sting of the bite was distant, and yet it set off a domino effect, the explosions of sensation intensifying until all of Quinton's nerves were on fire at once. Quinton's next stroke was angled to hit all the sensitive bundles of nerves inside Kit's sex. He thrusts, the scales along his shaft opening just as the spasms of pleasure raked through Kit's body.

Kit shattered in Quinton's hold and he shattered alongside her, the dizzying wave of molten pleasure coursing through him so intense it bordered on pain.

It was all he could do to hold on and keep them both from collapsing to the floor. Kit's responsive body spasmed in his arms, coming a second time with just the slightest shift to press against her sensitive nub. It felt good to be able to give her that, and better still to feel Kit falling limp against him, trusting Quinton to keep her safe as strength and magic drained away.

And then it was over.

Quinton carried the still dazed Kit to the bed and set her on the lumpy mattress. Her naked body was covered with sweat, and some of the blood that had slickened his skin had rubbed off on her. He adjusted his britches back into place and closed the window, drawing the curtains over the glass planes.

Kit watched him wearily. Satisfied but not relaxed. Not by a long shot.

He couldn't fault her for that. What they'd just done, it wasn't coupling—it was rutting. The fact that Kit's body had craved it as much as his own didn't change that fact. Nor did it diminish how drained Kit had to be or how sore he'd no doubt left her. Both from the pounding inside, and the slamming about that had come earlier. But what else could one expect when they were mated to him? If Quinton had ever been capable of being kind and gentle—the sort of male that Kit deserved—he wasn't now. Hadn't been for a long long time.

He at least had enough decency left to acknowledge that he'd made a literal bloody mess of Kit and should probably do something about that. Fetching the washbasin and a pitcher, Quinton set both beside Kit's hip. He didn't bother with explaining the obvious as he ripped a swath from the sheet to use as a washcloth and surveyed the damage. In addition to the others' rubbed off blood, fresh marks now covered Kit's smooth skin. Scrapes from the wall, floor and *him*.

The hour Quinton had spent away from Kit, tracking, interrogating and ending the two drunken guards who'd tried to kill her, had driven him mad—though dealing out their final blows had been a consolation prize. Quinton killed often. He never enjoyed it. But this night, he had. He'd have taken longer with the pair if he'd not been so desperate to get back and ensure his mate was alright.

Mate. Rutting hell.

And now that said mate was securely beside him, Quinton still didn't know the answer to that. Was Kit alright? Could she ever be now?

Holding the washcloth like a dagger, Quinton attacked the grime, sweat and blood covering Kit's collarbones. That she let him do it without argument was a mark of how spent she was. For a few minutes, the sound of cloth dipping into water and sliding along skin was the only one in the room aside from their quiet breathing. Finishing with Kit's shoulders, Quinton wiped down her arms, lingering on the slave mark her former masters had branded into her skin. Two overlapping circles, forming a small diamond at their intersections. The mark was red now, from where Kit had been scratching at it.

One day, Quinton intended to find whoever put that mark on her and remove their heart.

Tonight was for other things though. "Do you still intend to compete in the Equinox Trials?" he asked.

Kit took a moment to focus on him, the haze in her eyes disappearing. "Why wouldn't I?" She huffed in annoyance. "It was a good time, Quinton, but you didn't actually rut my brains out."

Quinton clenched his jaw. The notion of bringing his mate into a cesspool of people intent on killing her—for reasons that ranged from personal preference to collateral damage—sat with him about as well as a handful of explosives.

"Has something changed in the past hour that I'm unaware of?" Kit asked, sitting upright. "Is King Ettienne no longer the last line of defense keeping the immortals on this side of the world from using humans as their own personal stable of domesticated beasts?"

"No one's politics have changed," Quinton ground out.

"Maybe it's no longer vital that Ettienne's sons win the Equinox Trials and obtain the fertility elixir then?" she asked. "Has the threat to his rule disappeared while we were busy with other things?"

"Maybe you've forgotten that King Ettienne was the one who ordered me to kill you," Quinton tossed the washcloth into the basin and threw up his hands. "Or that his trusted guards attempted as much all on their own."

"And yet here I am."

"Oh for stars' sake." Quinton shook his head, starting to move away until his attention snagged on the mating bite mark he'd left on Kit's breast. Blood still trickled from the puncture wounds and stars, he liked the sight of it there, on Kit's flesh.

With the mating bond snapped into place, Quinton couldn't understand how he'd ever been able to breathe without the life-tether that now connected them. The bite mark was living proof that what Quinton felt now was both real and permanent. Which was good for him, but not so much for her. On second thought, it probably wasn't good for him either, if how the evening was progressing was any indication.

Either way, he could do nothing about the bond—that was permanent. But he could probably erase the bite mark, so at least she wouldn't have to see it in the mirror each time she changed.

Putting a hand on Kit's skin, Quinton fed a tendril of magic into the wound.

Kit swore at healing's burning pain, shoving his hand away with surprising strength. "Don't ever do that without asking again."

"Really?" Quinton cocked a brow. "Of everything that just happened, *that's* what you find most offensive?"

He examined his handiwork, bracing for the sight of smooth skin that hid his claim. The wound had closed, but instead of disappearing, the bite mark remained there, now a puckered slightly silver scar. That was unexpected.

Kit's face was unreadable as she ran her finger over the mark. "That was the one part of this whole evening that I actually understand," she confessed with equal parts resignation and annoyance.

She motioned for him to turn his back to her while she cleaned herself the rest of the way. Quinton obliged, wisely not pointing out the absurdity of modesty at this point. The bed creaked behind him as Kit rose to her feet.

"And what happened to your resolve about not healing humans anymore?" she asked into his back. "I'm certain I heard you say something idiotic to that effect after Cordelia died."

He crossed his arms. "My resolve bowed to the reality of being near a human who baits injury with her every breath."

"Did you just blame *me* for what happened?" Kit's voice rose with incredulity.

"So you didn't lunge at me first?" The tips of Quinton's scales turned a shade of irritated red. He was a predator. There was only so much he could do when a little mortal bit of prey was actively baiting a hunt. "Was it someone else who'd—"

"-I didn't say that." Her words were clipped. The floorboards creaked as Kit moved about the small room to dig out fresh clothes. By the time Quinton had enough with staring at the door and turned around, she was already buttoning up a drab gray dress. The garment hugged her curves deliciously despite having been tailored for someone else.

Lips pursed, Kit focused on the last of the buttons. "I… I don't know what happened," she said finally, not looking at him. "I couldn't think straight. Not about anything beyond, well, you were there. You know."

He did.

Quinton sighed. "It was a frenzy. A primal drive to fight or rut. It's a dragon thing. So no, don't ask me why you felt it. I have no idea. Nor do I know why I saw flashes of silver dancing in your eyes as I took you."

"There was magic in my eyes?" Kit wobbled slightly as she

set the wash basin and pitcher of water back atop the dresser.

Quinton barely held himself back from grabbing her elbow. "Yes."

Kit rubbed her face. "And this primal frenzy thing, is it going to happen again?"

"I don't know. Probably."

"How often?"

"I don't know."

"Well, for how long are these random *rut-me-now* instincts going to hijack my common sense?"

"I don't—" Quinton cut off as Kit twisted around and jabbed a finger into the middle of his chest.

"Don't you dare say you don't know," she snapped at him. "What *do* you know?"

That I'm an asshole who's just filled a jagged hole in my soul by ripping off a piece of yours.

"That you ask too many questions." Spinning on his heel, Quinton plucked his discarded shirt from the floor, then wadded it back up for disposal. The garment was beyond saving and he'd not thought to bring extra clothes along. His cloak would have to do for the ride back and then some. If he and Kit would be infiltrating the trials, they had to get her into the pledge ball unnoticed first. A ball that was to take place in the Massa'eve palace, ruled over by the very same king who ordered Kit dead. To top it off, they had about eighteen hours to accomplish it all.

Brilliant.

Muttering a string of curses, Quinton made use of the wadded up shirt to wipe himself down. Most of the blood on him was from the two guards he'd killed but some still trickled from the arrow he'd taken. The shot had been shallow and sloppy, and if Quinton hadn't already killed the guards he'd have sent them on their way just for their drunken incompetence.

"Why are you rubbing blood all over your chest?" Kit demanded, her lip curling in disapproval as she surveyed Quinton's efforts. Shaking her head, she ripped a clean swath of cloth from the destroyed sheet and pointed to the dresser. "Sit."

"I've got it." Quinton said, but did as he was told.

Pouring clean water over the cloth, Kit cleaned the wound with a gentleness that was at odds with her irritated expression.

Her citrus and cinnamon scent caressed Quinton's senses and, despite the sting of contact, Kit's touch felt healing. As if each brush of the cloth touched deeper than the torn flesh. No one had touched him that way. Not ever. The urge to lean into her touch, or better yet, to bury his face in Kit's hair and inhale her scent, was near impossible to resist.

Quinton pulled away.

"Don't you dare move," Kit snapped at him, her eyes flashing with fury. "Not a single stars' damned muscle," Kit continued through clenched teeth. "I want this to hurt."

He grunted uncommittedly but stayed still while Kit bound a makeshift bandage over his chest. He considered assuring her that if his plan to get them into the pledge ball worked, there would be plenty more bleeding gashes on his flesh, but despite her very own claim that she wanted him hurt, *she* was the one who flinched each time the wound was touched.

"That's as good as it's getting. Don't lose the dressing," Kit said, finally stepping away to examine her handiwork. The bandage was snug, its ends tucked neatly under the binding. "I expected it to be deeper."

"Yirel and Jared thought they were shooting a human and were too drunk to pull the bow properly," Quinton said tartly. "Plus, I heal quickly."

Not this quickly, though. The mating bond was doing something to him on the physical level too, but he couldn't understand—much less try to explain—what it was. He gestured to the bandage. "You didn't need to do all this."

"I don't have a lot of clothes and don't need your blood ruining the dress." Kit waved her hand along the well-worn garment. "I'm not sure what attire one wears back to a palace from where she was banished on penalty of death, but there weren't too many choices in the pack." She paused. "Also... Thank you."

"For what?"

"For taking the arrow meant for me, for starters."

"That isn't something you thank a mate for," Quinton said. "There is no other way. There never will be for me."

"You know, from someone else that might sound romantic," Kit said dryly.

"I was simply stating a fact."

"I noticed." Shaking her head, Kit pulled her hair back and started braiding it with efficient strokes. Quinton had the sudden urge to braid it for her. He bet the hair would feel as silky against his hands as it looked. Kit pulled her shoulders back, reminding him of a warrior preparing for battle. "What do we do now?" she asked.

"We ride back to the capital. I'll need a new shirt. And we need to stop in on a friend of mine." That last one was key. Quinton's entire infiltration plan relied on Autumn's help, which wasn't a position he liked being in but was the best of bad choices.

"Friend? I didn't think you knew what the word meant, much less had one."

Quinton shrugged one shoulder. Most of Massa'eve would agree with Kit's assessment. Hell, even his brothers would. But Autumn wasn't from this continent and she wasn't just a friend. Lady Autumn, sister to the king of the Slait Court, renowned scholar and visiting emissary was one of the few people in the world who knew of Quinton's *other* duties to the crown—those of a spymaster. It took one to know one.

Little as Quinton liked the idea of bringing more people into the deception, he knew when he was out of his depth. And getting his newly bonded, very mortal, mate into a ball that Ettienne was hosting? That was certainly in the deep end. Quinton pulled his cloak over his shoulders. "We will need help getting into the palace unnoticed."

"Aren't you mythically good at unnoticed?" asked Kit.

"I am. But I don't usually have a human tagging along."

"Sorry for slowing you down."

"I'll have to get used to it."

Kit shook her head. "One day, I'm going to murder you in your sleep."

CHAPTER 3

Kit

Though I knew we'd need to ride through the night to make it back to the capital, I still wince as Quinton swings me onto the horse, a massive beast named Rook that's as black as the night around us. Rook dances immediately, clearly as aware of my inexperience as I am. The saddle leather is slippery beneath my thighs and I struggle to find a secure grip without the aid of stirrups, which are set to Quinton's height.

Fortunately for both me and Rook, Quinton swings behind me a moment later, his body a solid line of warmth and stability against my back. One of his arms snakes around my waist, securing me to him, while the other takes the reins. I try my best to hide how comforting I find the power in his hold but Rook has no such scruples and immediately calms from an irritated prancer to docile steed.

Tell me how you really feel, horse.

The darkness seems to swallow us whole as Quinton nudges Rook forward, his hooves crunching on the gravelly path that leads out of the inn's stable yard. We're enveloped in the depths of a pine forest, the needles creating a muted, whispering sound as the wind sighs through them. Our only light comes from the moon above, its pallid glow illuminating the bark of the trees and casting ominous, skeletal shadows across our path. My skin prickles, raising the hair at my nape.

"Is it safe to ride at night?" I ask Quinton.

"No." He clicks his tongue and of course Rook listens, picking up a lope.

The path we take winds deep through the heart of the forest. Silver birches loom up on either side, their white bark glowing eerily. In the distance, the mournful call of a lone wolf reverberates, echoing in the stillness. I take comfort in it being a lone wolf instead of a pack of hungry coyotes.

After a while though, the scent of damp pine needles mingles with the musky aroma of horse sweat, grounding me to the night ride. Quinton's steady grip on the reins and his arm firm around my waist is a comforting anchor amid the eerie backdrop. Not that I intend to tell him that. I do however feel myself relax, especially as the road widens and flattens.

"You should sleep," Quinton says into my ear as we pass a

herd of deer grazing at a distance. The animals lift their heads as we pass, their eyes reflecting the moonlight with an otherworldly glow. They scatter as we get closer though, their swift, graceful movements painting a mesmerizing tableau against the night sky.

"Sleep? In the saddle?"

"Unless you've suddenly learned to fly, then yes."

"Well, I'm as likely to fly as sleep while atop this fiend."

Quinton breathes out an annoyed sigh, then shifts in the saddle, changing the reins to his other hand while he adjusts me against him and covers us both with his cloak. Then he mutters something to Rook and the horse's gait changes to an even, steady canter. The rhythmic cadence reminds me of being rocked.

"Sleep," Quinton orders again. "You are no good to anyone exhausted tomorrow."

I'm about to protest again, but then I feel a soft vibration against my back. A quiet soothing purr that I didn't know this dragon prince was even capable of. I'm still clinging to that surprised thought when the allure of much needed rest takes me.

By the time the horse's slowing gate nudges me awake, the first wisps of dawn are already breaking through the horizon and the scents of Massa'eve's marketplace overpower the faint sweetness of the mount's sweaty coat.

"This isn't the palace," I mutter, rubbing my face. We are on a narrow road dividing the market stalls and their early to rise owners from establishments that seem not to have gone to sleep to begin with. Sounds of various revelry, from rowdy songs and clinking tankards to more overt sounds of rutting escape various buildings, all of which Quinton navigates around with familiar ease.

"Very astute." Quinton pulls up next to a chocolatier of all places, exchanging coin for a wrapped package without bothering to dismount—or explain what he is doing—then points the horse toward a two-story building that's tucked away neatly on an adjacent side street.

A discreet polished brass sign names our destination as the *Silken Oasis*, the black exterior gilded with golden accents separating it from other establishments. Quinton dismounts smoothly then lifts me down from the saddle, my legs nearly giving out upon contact with the ground. Quinton pulls me back against his chest.

"I just need a moment," I mutter.

"You need to eat."

"I don't think that helps with gravity." I frown at the heavy door to the *Oasis* while Quinton hands the horse's reins to a hostler. "Also, this doesn't look like a diner. Where are we?"

Quinton opens the door, then pulls away a set of heavy velvet curtains. Only then do I mark the sounds of soft music coming from inside, mixing with the scent of burning incense and coquettish giggles. Another set of several curtains later, we enter a spacious antechamber decorated in orange and yellow hues. Several sconces bathe the space with warm dim lights, wisps of smoke flowering in the brighter patches. A side table and a pair of pillowed benches frame the space, leaving plenty of room in the middle while the wall holds paintings of enamored couples that leave nothing to the imagination.

I pull out of Quinton's hold and turn to him. "Did you just bring me to a brothel?"

"I did."

I rub my face. "Why?"

"To see a friend."

"I'm sure he'll be delighted to see you just now," I say. "Especially with me in tow."

"She."

Oh good. Quinton's friend is one of the women plying her trade here. Exactly who I want to be meeting within hours of becoming a prince's mate. Before I can press him on the details of what is clearly a brilliant plan, a flock of scantily clad females float into the alcove, their alluring smiles freezing on their faces the moment they behold Quinton.

"My prince," the lead girl says with a hasty courtesy. Her gaze brushes over my travel-stained clothes, clearly finding both it and me wanting. "It is an honor—"

Quinton's hand tightens possessively in the middle of my back. "Tell Nadine I require her services."

"You can tell me yourself." A female who would be in her fifth decade if she were mortal strides into the antechamber, carrying an aura of authority along with her ageless beauty. The smile she gives Quinton, and then me, has a hint of unexpected warmth. Striding over to us, Nadine kisses Quinton on both cheeks. I'm not sure whether I'm more shocked by her audacity or the fact that Quinton lets her do it.

"I was wondering when I'd have the pleasure of your company again," Nadine says. "But I gathered it would be tonight."

"And why is that?" asks Quinton.

"Because you weren't here yesterday, of course," her eyes sparkle with amusement. "And there are only so many hours left before all the eligible males are off beating their chests at the proving grounds. I might be a little isolated, but I do know some things that happen."

"You know everything that happens, Nadine. I'm looking for—"

"I know who you are looking for. Back room. Honestly, the sooner you can convince her to take her leave the happier my patrons will be. She's cleaned out some of my best cheaters. None of them have yet figured out what she has up her sleeve or how she puts it there—truth be told, I think that disturbs them as badly as the coin they are losing."

Quinton presses a pouch of what I'm sure is gold into Nadine's palm. "For your troubles."

"I'd rather you tell me what she is doing with the cards."

Quinton snorts. "Counting them. All of them. Even the stacked decks you are using."

"Ah." Nadine's brows raise with respect. Then her attention slides back to me. Beside the put together immortal and her perfectly sculpted charges, I feel like a stray kitten Quinton dragged in. Nadine inclines her head toward me. "I don't believe we've been introduced."

"She's mine," Quinton replies.

"Clearly." The corner of Nadine's mouth seems to be fighting off a smile.

"I'm Kit. And honestly, I'm as confused as you are about why I'm here."

Nadine's answering laugh is music incarnate. "No, my dear. I am most certainly less confused than you are. Or him. Whatever he says, don't let him convince you that he's—"

"That's enough," cutting off Nadine, Quinton starts to herd me to the next set of curtains.

"One other thing," Nadine calls. "Night's Veil is not to be found all of a sudden. What little there is is going at ten times the cost. And I've not heard of any arrest by the city guard."

Quinton pauses. "So, someone is buying up the supply."

Nadine spreads her hands.

"What is Night's Veil?" I ask.

"A key ingredient in a rare poison," Quinton says. "Tasteless and nearly clear except for an oily sheen. It induces body paralysis without affecting the mind. It's used to rig fights, with the victim remaining unaware. Correct dosage is critical, so it takes skill to administer—and there is no antidote if you get it wrong."

"You know a lot about poisons," I say.

Quinton raises a brow. "I kill people for a living, human. Let's go."

With that warm ending to the conversation, Quinton nudges me forward through the curtains. We make our way through the *Oasis,* past several large pleasure halls with fae of both genders in various states of undress and wits, to a door hidden behind an ordinary looking tapestry.

There is nothing ordinary about the room beyond however. Following Quinton inside, I'm immediately enveloped in a sultry haze of candlelight and rich, aromatic smoke. The walls, cloaked in plush, dark velvet drapes, muffle the sounds of the bustling brothel beyond. At the center of the room, a round, ebony card table seats four people—three male, one female.

Pushing me behind him, Quinton strides toward the players. We are two steps behind the female's chair when a small line of fire erupts in front of Quinton's boots, halting our progress.

"Not interested," she calls, not bothering to turn around.

One of her companions, a well-dressed male with a pile of gold coins to match the expensive cut of his clothes, leans back in his chair. "I wouldn't be so quick to decide, my lady," he croons. "You might like what you see."

"Does it have a cock?" she asks.

The male's gaze brushes along Quinton. "Oh, I think it does."

"Then I'm not interested. If you are, please indulge yourself elsewhere."

"Yes, please do," Quinton says dryly. "Game's over. Stop toying with your food, Sparkle."

The fire disappears at once, and the woman—who I presume is Sparkle—slides off her chair. She is smaller than I expected, a petite blond fae with hair in too many braids to count and a colorful dress that shows off a bare midriff. She's also barefoot. Surely this can't be the Lady Autumn of Slait Court Quinton had told me we needed to meet. Seeing us, the woman's full mouth slips into a smile. "Silver!"

Sparkle? Silver?

Still at the table, the male who'd spoken earlier reaches for Sparkle's cards. The cards go up in flame the moment he touches them, making the male pull back with a yelp.

"Hands to yourself," Sparkle calls over her shoulder. "Next time, I'll set your favorite part on fire."

"We need to talk," Quinton tells her.

With a sigh, she waves her hand, dismissing her playing companions. They grumble but leave. I briefly wonder if I shouldn't sculk out right along with them, but Quinton catches me around my waist and brings me to stand in front of him before I can take a step.

"Autumn, Kitterny," Quinton says. "Kitterny, Autumn. Appearances aside, Lady Autumn is the visiting dignitary from the Slait Court in Lunos's northern continent. Her sister-in-law is Queen Leralynn, who you've likely heard about. Autumn, this is Kitterny. My... mate."

Autumn's glances at me. "My condolences, Kitterny."

I can't stop a snort and she grins in response, making me like her immediately.

"I presume you interrupted my last evening of freedom for a reason?" she asks Quinton.

"Indeed." With the others gone, we settle around the now empty card table, with me trying to disappear into the rich chair while Autumn studies Quinton expectantly. Reaching into his satchel, Quinton pulls out the wrapped package he'd gotten from the chocolatier. "Peace offering," he says. "For leaving without saying anything the last time."

Autumn unwraps the package, her smile returning at the sight of a dozen chocolate spheres. She pops one into her mouth, her eyes closing in bliss. "Mmm." She moans indecently and pushes the box toward me. "You must partake. Not that it means I forgive him, but I'm not dumb enough to say no to good chocolate."

Quinton ducks his face. I think he is actually happy to have pleased Autumn and is embarrassed about it. Or else he is just visualizing himself dismembering random people. With Quinton, it really is difficult to tell. About as difficult as getting a straight answer about what we are doing here at all.

"Not that it isn't an honor to meet you, Lady Autumn, and stars know I have so many questions I'd love to ask," I say carefully, "but..."

"But the pledge ball for the trials starts at six o'clock this evening," Autumn says. "And I imagine this genius thinks I can do something for you two between now and then?"

"Can you?" Quinton asks.

"Depends on what it is," Autumn says. "I'm on the wrong continent to hide your mate for you while you try to keep some poor human alive long enough to breed her."

I wince. Autumn is... direct.

"Plus," Autumn continues, "my official role in Massa'eve includes observing the trials, so I'll be as entangled as you are. Well, not as entangled, but you understand my drift."

"We don't need to keep Kit from the trials," says Quinton. "We need to get her into them."

"Come again?" Autumn freezes with a chocolate halfway to her mouth. "Because I thought I just heard you say that you want to bring your mate *into* a brutal proving grounds, where she'll be tormented and likely killed."

"I didn't say 'want'," Quinton says. "Do you imagine I like this idea?"

"The idea is actually mine," I confirm.

Autumn finishes her chocolate as she weighs me with her gaze. "I take it back. You two are meant for each other. Start at the beginning and start talking." She waves toward me. "You. If we wait for Quinn to find enough words he is willing to part with, the trials will be over."

CHAPTER 4

Tavias

"**G**ood morning, Your Highnesses." The guards at the entrance to the great hall at the Massa'eve palace touched their fists to their chests and returned to attention.

Tavias weighted each of them with his gaze, knowing that Cyril was doing the same behind him. The inspection before a large event was routine, but the event itself—a pledge ball that would commit all contestants to the authority of the priests of Orion and the strange magic of the trial grounds—was anything but. Nothing could be permitted to go wrong tonight, and everything had the potential to.

"Whose idiotic idea was it to make the pledge ball into a

masquerade?" Tavias demanded. "There will be enough murder in the air without adding masks to the mix."

"It's tradition," Cyril replied with infuriating calm.

"It's an idiotic tradition." Tavias growled under his breath. Not only were costumes a security risk, but there seemed little point in pretty dresses and ethereal music when everyone knew that the attendees were out for blood. There was only one prize after all, one dose of the fertility elixir to be had. Quietly taking out the competition before the trials even began would be a tempting move for anyone with few scruples.

In fact, Tavias was certain that their cousin Geoffrey had been behind Cordelia's death a few weeks ago in an attempt to prevent Tavias's pack from entering the trials at all. It would have been a smart move, if it had worked. Geoffrey's father—Tavias's uncle—Salazar was quietly stirring a rebellion against the throne. If Geoffrey's pack won the trials and the elixir, it would go a long way toward swaying people toward Salazar's flag.

Dragon kind was dying out, after all. And the situation was dire enough that the only hope left was in superstition and prophecy.

A prophecy that Kit, with her lively brown hair and mind magic instead of air magic, did not fit at all.

"From distant lands, a mortal strays, with locks of white and air that plays," Tavias uttered under his breath. "Thus rises one that's strong and true, who'll conjure life her soul imbued."

"Her spirit fierce, her power vast, her fate entwined with dragons' past," Cyril picked up just as quietly. "Their numbers scarce, their hopes forlorn, for generations hatchlings mourn. Until the dragons forge a bond, a unity that grows beyond. With only her shall dragons find, a future thriving and entwined."

Tavias rubbed his face with his hands, the thought of Kitterny ripping open the unhealed wound inside his heart. "Is it selfish of me to mourn that she doesn't fit the prophecy, when not fitting it means that she gets to stay safe?" Tavias asked his brother softly enough to not be overheard.

"Yes," Cyril answered without hesitation. "The trials are nothing but torment and death for most of the humans. The nymph deserves a safer fate than that."

Tavias nodded his agreement. As much as it hurt to have lost Kit, the important part was that she was safe. Wherever she was. Tavias's jaw tightened. He'd shaken down half the palace staff for information on the woman's whereabouts. The stories all matched. The captain of the guard confirmed orders for taking Jared and Yirel off the duty roster for a fortnight; the purser had records of drawing a fair sum of gold at Ettienne's request; even the kitchens reported packing food. No one knew where Kit was being taken, but everyone agreed that she had left with exactly the sort of provisions one would expect for a one-way journey of the type Ettienne had outlined.

Plus, they'd all felt the temporary pack bond with Kit snapping when she'd left the palace.

"Did you try reaching out to her?" Cyril asked.

Tavias knew he meant with his mind. When they were near, Tavias's magic could send words into Kit's mind. "Yes." He schooled his voice to professionalism. "But the communication had never been two ways. I'd have no way of knowing whether she heard me or not. Hopefully she heard nothing. Leaving was the smart choice for her."

"Yes." Cyril sounded as calm and certain as Tavias wished he felt.

"Exactly." He nodded to himself. It was hard to keep pretending that losing Kit was anything but agony, but it really was what was best for her. If Tavias were a better male, he'd feel guilty that another woman, a spare Ettienne had ensured was available, would take Kitterny's place. But he didn't. The woman, Fionna, would serve her purpose and Tavias would do his best to keep her alive. But he didn't feel anything one way or another about it. Or about her.

Perhaps that too, was for the best. Caring was a liability.

Tavias's gaze swept over the vaulted ceiling overhead, its sapphire expanse was interspersed with silver celestial symbols that served as reminders of the dragons' lineage—at least as far as myth was concerned. Tavias highly doubted any of them actually came from a constellation given life. If it were true though, maybe the stars could condescend and make a few more dragons the same way, instead of letting the race dwindle to extinction for a lack of pups.

"Should we inspect the mezzanine?" Cyril asked.

Tavias nodded and headed for the rounded stairs to the

second level, which ran the perimeter of the hall, making it a tactically sound vantage point for the guards. The strategically placed archways also provided quick access to the balconies overlooking the palace grounds and allowed for an efficient response to potential threats. This morning, the guards were already on duty though Tavias made a note to exchange some of the younger ones for more seasoned hands.

When it came to security and armies, Tavias felt utterly confident in his skill. The thought of one day taking Ettienne's throne though sat with him like sour milk.

Pushing away politics, Tavias turned to look down at the great hall, his hands tight around the banister. For anyone watching, he would look to be surveying the security of the dais, the obsidian platform housing the king's throne, and the newly built semi-circular platform for the priests of Orion who'd be accepting the pledge. But that's not where Tavias's mind was no matter how hard he tried.

"Did you feel... something?" Tavias asked his twin. "Earlier. In the wee hours past midnight."

Cyril jerked, spinning around too quickly to be casual. In his blue open tunic, he looked every inch the dragon he was, the true powerful heir to the Massa'eve throne. It had been decades since Tavias had seen Cyril pulsate with power, but Cyril had awoken on the Phoenix. It was difficult to overlook the fact that Cyril's power and confidence had returned when Kitterny had been with them. More difficult still to watch and worry whether that part of his twin would wither again now.

Cyril cleared his throat, the line of blue scales along his temple shifting toward purple. "I... I had a sudden need to take an ice bath," he said quietly. "Even after taking care of myself. For a time, it felt like -"

"A frenzy?" Tavias supplied.

"Yes. Except there was no one there."

"Right." Tavias pinched the bridge of his nose. "Let's hope whatever it was only touched us. The last thing we need going into the pledge ball is Hauck rutting with everyone in a nearby tavern."

"He didn't," said Cyril. "He was passed out drunk in his chamber this morning. The staff said he'd not left the entire night."

"Tavias. Cyril." Quinton's low voice sounded just a pace away. That he'd managed to get that close with neither of them noticing was equal part testament to the silver assassin's skill and reprimand to Tavias and Cyril's diverted attention.

"Want to tell us where you've been?" Tavias asked over his shoulder.

"No," said Quinton.

Tavias turned toward Quinton, letting his dominance flow through the pack bond. Tavias knew that Quinton had left the palace last night, though no one had actually seen him do so. That wasn't acceptable. This close to the trials,

Quinton needed to fall in line with the pack and stop with his lone dragon shit. "Tell us anyway," Tavias ordered.

"I had an errand to run." Quinton sounded bored.

"What kind of errand?"

"An Ettienne kind of errand."

Rut.

"Speaking of Ettienne," Cyril said, smoothly stepping into the conversation, "we owe him an apology. His heavy-handed antics aside, he did do right by everyone last night."

"Did he?" Quinton's voice was flat, but he accepted the pivot.

Cyril nodded, squaring his shoulders. "As Tavias and I discussed earlier, the last place Kitterny needs to be is on the trial grounds. Now that I've calmed enough to get my wits back about me, I find myself grateful for Ettienne ensuring she doesn't have to go there. More than grateful. And he deserves for us to acknowledge as much."

"Kitterny would have given us an advantage at the trails," Quinton said coolly, as if the wildcat in question was nothing more than a commodity. "We'd have a better chance at victory with her than any other human."

A fury simmered within Tavias at that, a seething pool that threatened to spill over. "May I remind you, that Kitterny risked her life to pull a venomous spike out of your dragon's hide," Tavias said too quietly for the anger inside him. "Treating her as a living being and not a weapon is the least you owe her." His fingers clenched reflexively at his sides and he shook his head in disgust. "Kit's life is worth more than an advantage at the trials. If you don't see that, I pity you."

Quinton cocked a brow. "What I see is weakness speaking for the heir apparent to the throne. It's your duty to put Massa'eve first, brother."

"Massa'eve first?" Tavias echoed. A low sort of growl filled Tavias's chest, his breathing turning shallow as each exhalation pushed against the growing rage. "*You* wish to lecture me on duty and commitment? Who do you think defends our land and people from the blight, while you are out playing with shadows? Who holds the line while you slink off to kill?"

"Kitterny—"

"No." Tavias cut Quinton off. Blood pounding in his head, Tavias stepped so close to Quinton that mere inches of crackling air stretched between them. "You don't get to speak of her. Ever. Not after the way you tormented her on the Phoenix for your own bloody -"

Quinton punched Tavias.

CHAPTER 5

Tavias

Quinton's fist landed on Tavias's jaw, the impact splitting both his lip and the last shreds of control he had over himself.

Tavias launched himself at his brother, slamming him into one of the marble pillars. Quinton grunted and swung, the air whistling with the speed of his punch.

Tavias pivoted, narrowly avoiding the blow. The relief was short lived as Quinton's next attack caught Tavias in the ribs. It bloody hurt. Not stopping for a moment, Quinton dropped low and savagely swept Tavias's feet from under him.

A muted thud sounded as Tavias went down, the thin rug offering no protection from the marble beneath.

"Stand down both of you." Cyril lunged between them.

Quinton shoved Cryil away without breaking stride just as Tavias jumped to his feet. If this was how Quinton wanted to play, then so be it. Spinning, he thrust the heel of his boot into Quinton's chest. Hard.

Quinton stumbled back into a pedestal holding the carved bust of their great grandfather. The satisfying grunt he let out was barely audible over the sound of the statue toppling to the floor. As it crashed, Quinton unleashed himself with a blur of movement, each attack pressing Tavias back, back, back. The thuds of Quinton's strikes against flesh and bone echoed through the hall, each one a metronome of a fury filled orchestra.

Red pulsed at the edge of Tavias's vision. Gritting his teeth against the onslaught, he saw his chance when Quinton pulled back his fist for another punch.

Tavias whipped around with a spinning roundhouse kick, the toe of his boot connecting with Quinton's face.

Quinton's head snapped to the side. There was the distinct sound of cracking bone and a spray of blood making an arch in the air. Yet, the silver dragon barely flinched. He wiped the back of his hand across his face, smearing the red liquid across his cheek. Then, with a roar, he launched himself at Tavias, their bodies colliding with the force of two charging bulls.

Cyril was shouting something in the background, but Tavias couldn't care less what it was.

Quinton kicked. Tavias sidestepped the attack but was

suddenly jerked around as his foot caught the edge of an ornate rug. Momentum carried Tavias backwards, but he managed to grab Quinton as he stumbled.

Tavias's back hit the mezzanine guardrail. His world tilted, the momentum carrying both him and Quinton along in an unforgiving arch. Then they were both over the edge of the banister, falling onto the pristine ballroom floor beneath.

Tavias could probably have landed on his feet if he wasn't still trying to punch Quinton even midflight. But he was. So, the pair of them crashed down together in a heap, rolling apart with bloody snarls.

A female gasp sounded from the other end of the hall, followed by the sounds of breaking glass.

Still on his hands and knees, Tavias lifted his head to find Fionna—the pack's new bride to be—standing amidst a mess of shattered porcelain and spilt tea she must have been carrying. The human's skin was blanched white, matching the marble floor. Her gaze followed the blood dripping from Tavias's lip to the polished stone.

A few paces away, Quinton crouched on one knee, a snarl still on his face as he set his own broken nose back into place with a brutal efficiency that made Tavias wince.

Silence followed.

If Kitterny were here, she'd have yelled at all of them to pull their heads out of their asses. For all her residual timidity when it came to herself, she would become a force of nature when she thought the pack was in danger. Hell, the wildcat would go toe to toe with dragons when she thought they were being idiots—and Tavias knew they were being idiots just now.

A part of Tavias was disappointed when Fionna showed no such inclination.

Gathering herself together with clearly trained self-control, the pretty blond woman curtsied, as if she'd walked in on them having crumpets instead of a brawl.

"My deepest apologies for my clumsiness, my princes," she said, her voice polite and agreeable despite the fear filling her scent. "I see I have intruded at a bad time. May I clean this up now, or would you prefer I return later? Or perhaps I might fetch you something else meanwhile?"

Cyril vaulted over the banister from the mezzanine, landing near Tavias.

"Good morning, Fionna," Cyril said diplomatically. "There is no need to trouble yourself on either of those accounts." He efficiently issued orders to a guard to send for a cleaning crew, which gave Tavias the time he needed to get to his feet and straighten out disheveled clothes.

"Hello, Fionna," Tavias said. He was still out of breath, but made an effort to sound cordial for the girl's sake. It wasn't her fault that she was here, after all. Or that Quinton was an asshole. And she was clearly trying to be whatever it is she thought the pack wanted.

Fionna had been the only passable option of the three women Ettienne had brought. Of the two others, one hadn't stopped weeping the entire time, and the other lost her wits and tried to stab Quinton. He'd killed her before the blade touched his skin.

Tavias cleared his throat. "What are you doing here?" he asked their new bride apparent.

"I thought you might wish for something refreshing as you went about your duties, my prince," Fionna said with another curtsy.

"We do have servant staff in the palace," said Tavis. "At least we did the last I checked."

He hadn't spoken harshly, but Fionna lowered her head, chastised. "Yes, of course. I will leave such duties to those who know you better and be more mindful of your need for privacy in the future. I only... I only wished you to know that I'm available for whatever you might need."

Tavias opened his mouth to control the damage but Quinton chose that moment to insert himself.

"Available are you? For whatever we might desire?" Spreading his shoulders, Quinton brushed past Tavias and Cyril to advance on the poor human. Blood from Quinton's broken nose still covered his face and clothes, and he made no move to tamp down on the power emanating from him. His scales were up, strands of bloody hair savagely framing his violence-filled face. "What if what we desire is you?"

"What in the rutting hell?" Cyril muttered, but Fionna's fingers were already at her dress, finding hidden ties with practiced efficiency.

"Then I will be honored to be of service, of course," Fionna responded at once, her voice barely wavering. Before Tavias could utter a sound, the gown she wore fell in a pool to the floor, leaving the woman in nothing but a set of lacy underthings that caressed her body. She was well put together. Beautiful even.

Yet the thought of taking her filled Tavias with no desire whatsoever.

Quinton grabbed Fionna's chin, lifting her face toward his. "Do you wish to be taken by us?" he demanded, his voice low.

"Of course, my prince," she answered quickly, as she'd obviously been taught to do. "Unless of course you would prefer to be serviced in another way? I have been taught several ways of bringing pleasure to a dragon."

Quinton stepped back in disgust.

"I am also happy to learn anything new you would prefer," Fionna said, a hint of desperation tinging her voice for the first time. "It is truly an honor to serve Your Highnesses. My mother and sisters have all borne many children and I am certain I would bear many healthy pups for the pack. Please don't send me away."

"No one is sending you anywhere, Fionna," Tavias said, stepping in before Quinton decided to terrorize the poor girl again. Blight take him, they could do a lot worse for a human. Fionna was agreeable, eager to please, and, under-standable fear aside, willing to do everything required. Equally important, Tavias and the others would be able to think around her—with their heads instead of their cocks. "In fact, allow me to escort you to breakfast."

He held out his arm to lead Fionna toward the door, stopping only for a moment to address Quinton. "Get your shit together before the masquerade tonight. And stay out of my sight until then."

CHAPTER 6

Kit

I'm still coming to grips with having been left with Autumn in a brothel, when one of the courtesans makes a final adjustment to Autumn's make-up and steps back to admire her work.

Autumn twirls, the fabric of her emerald green masquerade gown catching the air. "What do you think?" she asks me.

"You look gorgeous," I say honestly, watching her newly curled and pinned hair sparkle with the diamonds woven into it. Several of the *Oasis's* ladies have been fussing over Autumn and me for hours now, their skill enough to put any royal handmaiden to shame. "Every eye at the ball is going to be on you, mask or no mask."

Autumn's smile brightens and she bounces on her toes. "Now let's look at you. Spin around." She emphasizes the motion with her finger.

I turn like she had, albeit with less speed and grace. My own gown, put together with haste by several seamstresses on the *Oasis's* discreet payroll, is a carefully downplayed imitation of Autumn's own. Made to honor the Earth Court of Slait, the dress is a homage to a forest at dusk. It has a deep emerald bodice that hugs my figure and sparkles subtly under the lights. Lower down, the gown transitions to a skirt of softer hues, the earthy browns yielding to gentle, muted gold, reminiscent of the sun setting behind a woodland canopy. Light, delicate embroidery of vines and leaves and even a few gemstones sewn in as dewdrops pull everything together.

It's as unlike me as the bleach blond hair I now have braided behind me.

"Brilliant," Autumn declares. "Though it would be even more so if you stopped looking like you want to pick a wedgie."

She holds my mask out to me. Made of thin molded leather, it's designed to cover the top of my face and is painted in the same earthy hues as my gown—deep emerald, soft brown, and muted gold. A few delicate feathers at the edges both add a whimsical touch and flutter whenever I move. Most importantly though, the mask's wide wings are large enough to conceal my rounded ears.

Autumn checks the time. "Playtime is over, I'm afraid. Time to go put this hairbrained scheme into motion."

Hairbrained is a good way to describe Quinton's plan. I blow out a long breath, my stomach clenching as I fasten my mask into place and follow Autumn through an underground passage into a waiting carriage. Judging by the princess's confident steps, she's made this trip many times.

Well, obviously, since she is officially housed at Massa'eve's best inn, not a brothel.

"So you came to Massa'eve to observe the Equinox Trials?" I ask, as the carriage drives along a cobble-stone path.

"No, that's just a side interest," Autumn says easily. In the past few hours I've discovered Autumn to be wonderfully talkative—though only about topics of her choosing. She wouldn't tell me a word about how, or even where or when she and Quinton met. "I'm primarily representing the Slait Court in our hopes to establish closer relations with our far neighbors. But while I'm here, my scholar side demands indulgence."

"And the Equinox Trials have your interest?"

"Not so much the trials as these priests of Orion who run them. That, and the changing nature of the dragons' fertility." She speaks with such refined confidence that I'm starting to question whether I'd really seen her playing cards at a brothel a few hours ago. "Why do dragons need *human* women for example? Why not fae? And where are all the dames?"

"Dames?"

"Female dragons. Have you seen a single one around?"

I frown. "I didn't know there were female dragons."

"There aren't," Autumn confirms. "See my point?"

I don't really. If I can accept that immortal dragon shifters exist, accepting that they happen to also be male seems insignificant. Or maybe I'm just too nervous for critical analysis. I feel a slight sting and look down to realize that I've been itching the slave brand on the inside of my forearm again. Autumn seems to notice as well and frowns. I tug my dress sleeve over the irritated skin and focus on the approaching palace.

When the carriage finally comes to a stop, the door is swung open from the outside. Autumn regally accepts a waiting footman's hand to help her down and I do the same, always keeping a step behind the princess, the way a proper handmaiden would.

We walk together to the grand entrance and Autumn presents her invitation to the guards.

"Good evening, Princess Autumn. King Ettienne of Massa'eve welcomes you," the guard says. The mention of Ettienne's name reminds me of his promise to have me put to death if I ever return to the palace, but the guard gives me no more than a cursory look.

I guess that's the one bright side of Quinton's mission to kill me—no one is on the lookout for me.

Stepping into the grand hall for the first time, I nearly trip over my own feet. The place makes the receiving hall at

Agam estate, where I've spent most of my life, look like a child's playroom. The vaulted ceiling is a stunning canvas of sapphire and silver, the painted stars and celestial symbols twirling and shimmering as if alive. In the center, the dais with Ettienne's gold and ebony throne is mercifully empty, but the raised platform before it holds three males in priests' robes who look as intimidating as the flying dragons on the mural behind them. The priests' faces are shadowed by their hoods, but what little I can see of their skin is covered in tattoos.

"This way," Autumn says under her breath, guiding me toward a curving staircase to the white marble mezzanine that encircles the room. The open archways and balconies provide a view of the palace grounds and the hundreds of people dancing below. Gowns and masks twirl in perfect beat to the music of the ensemble at the far corner. It's all, well, beautiful and majestic and utterly out of my league.

I don't understand how the males imagined I would *ever* fit in here. Forget dancing, I couldn't even manage the heeled shoes these people are wearing. I know because we tried at the *Oasis*, until Autumn finally declared that a handmaiden who can't take three steps without falling on her face would be more conspicuous than one in less than ideal footwear.

Instinctively, I scan the dancers for my males. Despite the cursory costumes, finding Tavias is easy. His large body and preternaturally graceful movements would make him stand out on the crowded dance floor even if he wasn't wearing a glorious scaled tunic and twirling an equally glorious woman. The beauty in Tavias's arms who wears a gown of deep amethyst must be Fionna, the spare human Quinton told me the pack chose to replace me.

I watch her follow Tavias's lead through a complex spin, as if she'd been born to this. Hell, maybe she was. Prophecy and all.

My stomach lurches in unreasonable envy.

"This is a really bad idea," I say under my breath.

"Oh, it's absolutely terrible," Autumn agrees. "But given the dragons' declining numbers, none of the good ideas have worked out well, so there is that."

I open my mouth to correct Autumn's misunderstanding of my meaning, but decide against it. She's done so much, she doesn't need to hear me whine.

Forcing my attention away from Tavias and Fionna, who are now rotating around each other like vines in deference to the violins' rolling melody, I look for the others. I spot Hauck easily, busy with a chalice of wine and find Cyril a few moments later. The water dragon stands near his father's throne, his hands behind his back as he watches everyone and everything with a commander's competent eye. The aura of quiet power coming from Cyril is almost as strong as it had been on the Phoenix and seeing him like that fills me with pride.

What strikes me as odd though, is that none of them seem to be looking for me. Not even Hauck. Not even Cyril, after spotting Autumn on the mezzanine and giving her a respectful bow.

Something isn't right. My pulse skips. "Where is Quinton?" I ask.

"Behind you."

I startle at the sound of Quinton's low voice as he steps out of the shadows. He is dressed in black, the patterns of silver scales sewn along his coat looking more like armor than embellishment. Unlike the winged masks of most of the attendees, Quinton wears a tight band around his eyes—eyes that hold a promise of violence that no concealment can conquer. I don't immediately see weapons on him, but I'm sure he's armed. Not that the assassin needs steel to end life —and every particle of air around him seems to know as much.

Every particle except those belonging to Autumn, that is. The princess's eyes sparkle as she gives Quinton a formal curtsy that he returns with an equally proper bow. He doesn't look at me. Doesn't even acknowledge my presence. The bite mark on my breast is a whole other story. That flares, sending pulses of awareness through all my nerves. Especially ones low down in my belly.

"There are stairs beyond the privy doors," Quinton says quietly. He is speaking to Autumn, though the instructions are plainly intended for me. "Wait another half hour, then descend. You will see a door at the bottom of the stairs. It will appear to be locked. The handle is a decoy, as the door opens by a foot lever. Go inside and wait. Do you understand?"

"Yes," I say, though the sudden unwelcome onslaught of

desire is making it annoyingly difficult to concentrate on the instructions. I wish I was wearing a lighter gown, one that didn't run the risk of sizzling me alive in my own damn heat.

"Repeat the instructions back to me," Quinton orders. He gives no sign of feeling anything unusual, but the tips of his scales are changing color every few seconds. When I finish reciting the orders to his satisfaction, he gives a small grunt of approval. "Good," he says. "Once you get inside, just wait. I will bring Fionna there when it's time."

I clear my throat. "No disrespect Quinton, but perhaps the job of luring a woman into a dark corner might be better accomplished by Hauck or—"

"None of the others know the plan."

My face flies toward Quinton, forgetting that I'm supposed to be background decoration while my betters are speaking. "Please tell me that my hearing is off, because I thought you just said that none of the pack knows I'm here."

"I did."

Not my hearing then. Just Quinton's mind. I stare at him. "Are you rutting insane?"

"Tavias would not have gone along."

A wave of hurt races along my spine.

"They've realized that putting you into the very center of danger is the last thing any of them want," Quinton continues, pausing meaningfully. "And they aren't wrong, human."

In other words, I still have a chance to back out. I've had this conversation with Quinton and myself enough times to know that I don't want another round. I'm doing this. To

Quinton's credit, he doesn't push. I dislike many things about him, but he respects my choices.

Quinton inclines his head toward the dais with the priests. "In a little while the priests will start calling up packs to pledge themselves and accept the mark. You cannot be recognized until then. Once the runes are painted on your skin, you will be magically bound to the trials."

"The pack will scent me before that," I point out. "On our way to the dais if nothing else."

"At that point, you all will be in the public eye," Autumn says shrewdly. "They won't dare expose the truth lest they wish you executed outright. And once you are on the dais, Ettienne will have no sway."

"Correct," says Quinton.

I blow out a breath. Talk about a ruthless plan. I know Ettienne and Tavias will be furious—and rightfully so. All of them will be. When I imagined all this in my head, the welcome from the pack was a great deal warmer.

Quinton's gaze narrows on movement near the dais. I glance over to see that Ettienne has taken the throne and a dark haired male who bears a resemblance to the king is now kneeling before it.

"Salazar is here," Quinton says.

Ettienne rises to offer his brother a hand up, the pair looking like the best of allies. Except I know better. Salazar is plotting to take Ettienne's throne, and if his son Geoffrey's pack wins the trials, he'll likely have enough support from the people to start open rebellion. Behind Salazar, a pack that I presume to be Geoffrey's stands tall and proud in masquerade costumes made in imitation of rising serpents.

"Salazar is making little secret of his alliance with Nagaia and her Serpent Court, isn't he?" Autumn says.

"No, he isn't." Quinton's jaw tightens. "I need to go."

Despite his words, Quinton hesitates for a second, his gaze meeting mine and reigniting everything inside me. It truly is unfair for the stars to have made Quinton so damn beautiful, his every movement filled with a panther's grace and a dragon's power. His lips part slightly and my treacherous body tightens at the sight of the sharp canines. I swallow.

"Is there something else?" I ask.

"Don't die, human," says Quinton. "Tavias will want the pleasure of killing us both himself."

CHAPTER 7

Kit

The door to the small room opens on silent hinges, letting in the sounds of the ballroom beyond for the briefest of moments. My stomach jumps. The hour I've been here, waiting alone in the dark, has been one of the longest of my life—but the next one, might just prove longer.

In the soft light of my lantern, I see Quinton push a wide-eyed Fionna inside. A wave of confusion, obvious despite her winged mask, rolls over her as her attention lands on me. Then I feel the heat of Quinton's gaze and my mind goes blank at the palpable hunger there. The shadows themselves seem to crackle around us, and the pounding of a heart that I know isn't mine echoes through my chest.

Quinton swallows, his hand tightening on a shelf's edge with a white knuckle grip.

"How... How can I be of service to my prince?" Fionna asks, her voice breaking the silence.

Quinton ignores her. His mouth parts, the tips of his canines scraping against his lip. His costume, which was merely perfect amidst the backdrop of the ballroom, now seems an ethereal representation of a dragon made flesh. Midnight black, accented with armor-like scales along his spine and shoulders. Coupled with the predatory violence that radiates from Quinton's lithe movements, he is impossible to look away from.

"My prince?" Fionna asks again.

His attention still on me, Quinton waves his hand. "You explain."

"Why me?" I ask.

"Because the alternative is that I explain." His voice sounds low and steady, at utter odds with the pounding pulse that I know is his. "And I don't explain."

"Fair point," I agree, turning toward Fionna. The young woman is worrying her dress, but waits patiently otherwise. For someone who has no idea what's happening or why she's been pulled into a dark supply closet with a killer dragon prince and a strange woman in Slait Court colors, she is holding it together well. "Fionna—"

A gong sounds beyond the wall, cutting me off.

Quinton curses. "They are starting the pledge ceremony," he says. "Talk fast."

"I'm not the one who waited this long to get started."

"You have even less time now."

Turning my back to Quinton, I swing my attention to Fionna and survey her quickly. She is thinner and taller than me, but the clothes should fit. More or less. They'll have to.

"Fionna, my name is Kit. I'm not here to hurt you." I make my voice friendly despite the time crunch. "In fact, I've some good news—you need not go through the trials."

"Of course I do." Fionna's brow furrows. "I am to pledge in a few minutes."

"You won't have to go to the trials because I will take your place." I pause, searching Fionna's face for comprehension. "I will go in your place to the trials, and you will go free."

Instead of thanking me profusely, she twists to Quinton, her eyes wide. "Have I done something to displease you, my prince?"

"Yes."

"W-what have I done?"

"You exist," Quinton says.

"I don't understand."

He bares his teeth. "You. Exist. Your existence displeases me. Clear enough?"

"Oh for stars' sake!" I shove Quinton in the chest, which does nothing except make me feel better. Taking Fionna's hands in mine, I turn the confused girl toward me. "Don't listen to that asshole. You've done nothing wrong. This is good news. It means you are free to go where you will."

She stares at me, fear paling her already blanched skin.

61

"My family has already spent against the bridal payment. They'd be destitute if I failed to fulfill my duty."

Stars. Fionna is as much of a slave as I ever was. More. I've only had my own life to guard.

The gong sounds again, and I can see from the way Quinton's hands are twitching at his sides that he's about to lose his patience, strip Fionna bare and leave her here gagged.

"No return debt will be sought," I assure her, quickly explaining that she'll need to change clothes with me and find Autumn, who will get her the rest of the way out of the palace. "You choose what you do next. No dragon princes, no trials, no obligations except to say nothing of what's happened here."

She still doesn't move. "B-But what would I do?" she asks me so earnestly that it breaks something inside me. "I know nothing except how to please their highnesses. I've no other purpose."

"Blight take me." Quinton advances on Fionna. There is enough menace flowing from him that she steps away, her spike of fear so sharp that even I can scent it. Or is it me feeling Quinton's body again? *Shit.*

A growl rumbles deep inside Quinton's chest. "You want to please a dragon, girl? Well, here is how you bloody please me: find yourself a better purpose than dying at the trials for the sake of other peoples' problems. Understood? Either that, or I can snap your neck now and be done with it."

Well, that's another way of getting to yes. Fionna nods with what seems like reflex.

That's all the signal I need to start stripping out of my gown. The gong is sounding yet again beyond the wall, and the hum of the ballroom is falling quickly now. We are out of time for talk and I'm so focused on getting into Fionna's dress that I jump when her fingers close around my forearm.

"Your mark," she says. "I've seen it before."

I jerk my arm back, my jaw tightening for a moment. "Yes. I know. It's a slave brand."

"Oh, is it?" she shrugs, getting back to her own dress. "I didn't know. Our estate didn't keep slaves."

"Well, now you know."

"Strange."

I've neither time nor interest to find out what about my brand Fionna finds strange, because there is no more music at all coming from the other side of the door. No more dancing.

The moment the last lace button of my dress is fastened, Quinton leads me out into the eerily silent Great Hall. Except for the occasional quiet whisper or rustling silk, everyone's attention is rooted to the priests' dais. There are three priests of Orion there now, all in hooded robes. Their faces are tattooed with images of constellations, as if they wear a living map of the heavens on their skin.

As Quinton and I snake our way through the crowd, the middle priest steps forward. A pack of four shirtless dragon shifters and one fully dressed human woman are already kneeling on the hardwood of the dais.

"What's with the stripping?" I ask Quinton. With shirts off and masks on, the whole thing looks decidedly odd.

"Quiet," Quinton hisses back.

On the dais, the priest holds up a ceremonial dagger and a silver chalice with an image of a dragon's eye. The priest bares his forearm—which too is tattooed with constellation marks—and deftly slices the blade over his skin.

I flinch.

The priest spills several drops of his blood into the chalice, then proceeds down the line of the kneeling pack to draw a similar sacrifice from each of his five pledges. Each time a new drop of blood touches the silver, the dragon's eye pulsates with a flash of light.

"Have you come to stand before the Goddess Orion, Celestial Dragon who watches us always, to seek her permission to enter the Equinox Trials?" The priest's voice, filled with divine authority, resonates through the hall.

"We do," the dragon shifters answer as one. The woman with them follows along a moment later, but none of them pay attention to her.

"And, should she grant your request, are you ready to receive the Mark of Orion, which will bind you to her will, as delegated by her to my judgment, and mine alone?" The priest asks.

"We do," the group answers.

"Do you pledge yourself from the moment of your marking until I release you from the trials?"

"We do."

"Then so it shall be." Dipping the dagger into the chalice, the priest chants softly and draws a symbol in the air. The mark glows above the dais, and then again on the bare backs of the males. A similar mark glows on the woman's neck. That explains the dressing arrangements at least.

The dragons go rigid as the magic sears their skin, but the woman screams. Her howl of pain echoes from the fancy marble columns and statues until the mark settles, leaving a luminous tattoo behind.

"Orion has accepted your pledge," the priest announces as the pack on the dais removes their masks.

There is a scattering of applause but the competitors are mostly busy memorizing the faces of their foes. Probably cataloging potential weaknesses to exploit. I instinctively know the woman's scream marked her as easier prey and vow not to make a sound when my turn comes.

"Reconsider this, human," Quinton's near silent words tingle along my neck, the tension from his body vibrating my own. "You'll be hurt. Even if we win, you will be hurt."

"Interesting objection coming from you," I mutter.

"If you mean the Phoenix, I was simply demonstrating the dragons' nature," Quinton says with no hint of apology as another pack kneels before the priest. The woman with this lot is weeping openly and has to be held in place by two of the dragons.

I want to look away but make myself watch. Autumn and I counted thirty four packs at the ball today. Thirty four, all ready to kill each other for one vile of the elixir.

Mathematically speaking, more would die in the trials than would be born from the subsequent breeding, but math doesn't hold a candle to hope and competition. I'm proof of that.

A small puff of air from Quinton ruffles my hair. I have a feeling he wants to say something more about me reconsidering this and give him a warning look. I can't walk away. There are things bigger than us both at stake.

"...are you ready to receive the Mark of Orion, which will bind you to her will, as delegated by her to my judgment, and mine alone?" The priest's voice rises above the woman's sobs and fills the room. "Do you pledge yourself from the moment of your marking until I release you from the trials?"

"No!" The woman screams. One of the dragons slaps her across the face, leaving a bloody lip. The priest doesn't blink an eye. Her consent doesn't matter to him.

Quinton, get yourself and the human here now! Tavias's voice sounds in my mind. He sounds... Well, furious doesn't begin to cover it. My head swivels through the crowd, looking for the pack, but it's hard to see with everyone now packed tightly around the dais.

"You still have a choice," Quinton tells me. His voice is quiet and quick. "You can choose to send Massa'eve and its rites to rutting hell."

I raise my chin in answer, though I know there is no hiding my galloping heart, not from him. Still, in this moment I am more certain than ever in the one advantage I have over the woman weeping on the dais. Over all the humans here. "I know I have a choice," I tell him. "And I choose to stay and fight."

A thousand emotions dance over Quinton's usually stoic face, the tips of his scales shifting too quickly for me to follow. But at the end, the dragon prince gives me a barely perceptible bow that steals my breath. "It will be an honor to fight beside you."

Quinton! Tavias's mind shout is so loud it's actually painful. I am not sure how I'm hearing it at all since he is talking to Quinton, but it's always been that way with us, since that very first time I heard Tavias's voice in my head, giving an order to kill.

"We should find Tavias," I say.

Quinton's hand rests on the nape of my neck. "No. Not yet."

"Are you insane?"

"Clearly, yes."

Shit. Quinton is stalling. Making absolutely certain that by the time we are close enough for the others to realize the truth, there is no chance to undo this. I have to give it to him, once Quinton decides to do something, he commits—and lets the consequences be damned.

A fresh rush of nerves, ones that had been forgotten while I was watching the ceremony, grabs the forefront of my thoughts. As if the priest, the trials and Ettienne's death threats weren't enough to worry about, we are stretching Tavias's temper to homicidal.

There is a fresh scream, the Goddess Orion plainly caring

as little as the dragons as to whether the woman they hold consents to all that's involved, and a new set of five ascends the dais. The woman with them has cold steel in her eyes, smiling in satisfaction as she watches her predecessor being led away.

"That is Geoffrey's pack," Quinton tells me and somehow I'm not surprised one bit.

Quinton! We are next, you rutting asshole. Get here now or I will rip out your eyes and feed them to the sclices.

Quinton cocks a brow at me. "Alright human," he says. "Let's go see if Tavias's lightning doesn't bring this whole place down on our heads."

CHAPTER 8

Kit

"Where the hell—" Tavias's words freeze as I step out from behind Quinton, my masked face raised toward the pack leader. Tavias is half-way through removing his shirt, the intricate overcoat already folded neatly on a chair beside him, when the reality of my presence registers.

Disbelief flashes in his gaze, which turns too quickly to fury. Tension and magic crackle along Tavias's muscular body, as he no doubt realizes that nothing about our last minute arrival is accidental.

Sorry, not sorry.

Tavias straightens to his full height slowly, each muscle moving with tense, trained precision. I can't read the look he gives Quinton. It's the kind only brothers who've known each other since childhood can interpret. Quinton raises his chin slightly, his mouth in a hardline.

I clear my throat, reclaiming Tavias's attention. Despite my better reason, getting one over on him feels childishly good. Then my eyes narrow. "Is that... a swollen lip?" I ask him.

Tavias turns away, ignoring me in favor of surveying the ballroom.

"Oh, it's very much a swollen lip." Hauck answers for him, sliding up toward me. He is already shirtless of course and delighted mischief lights up every line of his face as brightly as anger still tightens Tavias's. "Wait until our shadow takes off his mask, too. His nose is a delight." Behind Hauck, one of the vases with flowers is surreptitiously starting to sprout extra leaves that unfurl provocatively. With only a pace of space remaining between us, Hauck scrapes his canines along his bottom lip. "Hello there, turnip."

It's hard to keep the grin from my own face, and I don't try. Before we can come together however, Cyril shoots out his arm, blocking our paths. Of the four princes, his face is the only one I cannot read at all. Right now, he is the embodiment of control, though only a fool would mistake his fluid motions and intelligent eyes for anything but deadly. His bare muscled torso has as many scars as Quinton's.

"This isn't the time," Cyril's voice is barely audible, his face schooled and taking in everything at once. "Close ties are a vulnerability that can and will be exploited. If you want her to stay alive, do not show undue affection." He surveys the dais as he speaks and, despite his mask, I know he is calculating the time we have until the priest calls our pack. Seeing if there is anything to be done to get me out of here.

There isn't. Quinton's timing ensured that.

Hauck huffs, but sticks his hands into his pockets. Despite standing still, he isn't *being* still though. His honed muscles shift beneath smooth skin, as do the scales that run along the midline of his body to disappear into the waistband of his trousers.

He follows my gaze and smirks.

Yeah. The ass bristled his scales on purpose. Like a peacock. A very powerful, immortal, killer dragon peacock.

"You are going to want to take the rest of that shirt off," Quinton tells Tavias, who still has one arm in a sleeve. "It's not a good look if you can't manage to get yourself undressed."

"Agreed." Ettienne's voice makes me jump.

Shit. My heart is slower to recover than the rest of me. I'd not seen the king approach and curse myself for not having been on the lookout for him. Between taking in the ceremony and anticipating Tavias's fury, I'd temporarily forgotten about the most powerful male in the entire dragon court.

His hands clasped behind his back, Ettienne weighs me with his gaze, his face the epitome of mild curiosity. My heart continues to hammer, remembering the death he'd promised if I were to ever speak to his sons again. A corner of my mind wonders if he might try to make good on that now, rather than be content with letting the trials take care of it.

"Interesting," Ettienne remarks with that causal grace that sends a chill down my back. "Do not take another step."

It takes me a moment to realize that the latter is addressed toward Quinton, who is indeed trying to blade his body between me and his father. Quinton's bare back is riddled with scars, which speak to more pain than I can imagine, given how quickly dragons heal. I've no doubt Ettienne's training is responsible for a fair share of those. Just as Ettienne is responsible for the ones on Cyril, having left him to an enemy court's inquisitors for disobeying orders.

"This is not the time to start wearing your weakness on your sleeve, Shadow," Ettienne advises quietly. "The other competitors will use it against you."

Following Ettienne's pointed gaze, my attention cuts to the dais, where the members of Geoffrey's pack are rising to their full height and pulling masks off their faces. None of them, including their woman, had made a sound as they were marked. Now they sweep their attention over the crowd, the predatory intent evident in their faces.

Geoffrey's attention stops on Tavias. There is an echoing similarity between the two males, with their wide angled jaws, impressive height, and shoulders broad enough to hold up the world. But where Tavias's scales are purple and his eyes fierce, Geoffrey emanates nothing but cold and blackness. Shifting his feet, Geoffrey seeks out Cyril next. He holds his attention there, a smile full of cruel satisfaction crossing his face as he subtly runs his hand over the scales decorating his costume. A reminder of the serpent court whose dungeons Cyril was held in.

"Prince Cyril," Geoffrey says with perfect politeness. "Allow me to introduce my bride apparent, Bianca."

Bianca stretches her neck and the newly tattooed collar there, as if showing off her plumage. Unlike the small bands around the others' necks, Bianca's tattoo covers all the skin from her collarbone to jaw, the beautiful twirls of black ink contrasting against her snow white hair.

"It is a mark of Orion's favor," Ettienne advises quietly.

"Oh, my apologies," Geoffrey snaps his fingers and cringes in a show of contrition. "It's not you in charge any more is it? I meant no disrespect, cousin Tavias. With all of you running away from the throne, it's hard to keep track of who has the burden at the moment."

Predictably, lightning crackles over Tavias's scales and he takes a step toward the dais.

Less predictably, Ettienne calls him off.

Reclaiming control of the proceedings, the priests motion for Geoffrey to clear the dais. The crowd parts to let the pack off, and it's only because I'm watching Bianca instead of the dragons that I notice her slip her hand into the slit of her dress. Steel flashes.

"What—" My words are cut short as Bianca's knife flies into the crowd. In the next moment, it's buried deep in the chest of the weeping girl from the pack who'd pledged earlier. Blood spurts onto the girl's pretty dress, her quiet sobs turning to gurgles. Then she is on the floor, her life draining out onto the marble.

The pack who'd brought her snarls, but Geoffrey's laughter is the more contagious sound.

"It is never too early to cull the weak," Geoffrey calls, eliciting applause. He turns to the dais, and bows low. "My pack is pleased to make the equinox's first offering to Orion," he tells the priest.

The priest bows. *Bows.* As if the scared girl whose life Bianca just extinguished was never worth any more than a blood offering.

You are dead. Tavias's voice booms in my head so loudly that it hurts. He is glaring at Quinton and I am not sure whether he remembers that I can hear him too. Or cares. The mark on my breast tingles, reminding me that Tavias doesn't know half of what's happened in the last two days. *Did you think bringing her here—*

"I imagine he knows exactly what he did," Cyril interrupts in that quiet controlled voice of his. "And I support your decision to rip him limb from limb for it—but in private. Geoffrey is watching our every breath. And there is no time now regardless."

The gong sounds, the priest calling Tavias's name and just like that all the squabbling and threats disappears into irrelevance. It's our turn.

I am so nervous that I'm numb as I ascend the wooden dais beside the rest of the pack, Tavias and Quinton kneeling on either side of me. Against the din of the crowd and the image of the frightened girl's blood spilling onto the marble floor, the priest's words sound like a foreign language. I've not heard of Orion before today and vaguely wonder why a goddess who watches over the dragonkind's fertility would have so little value for life as to be pleased by blood sacrifice.

Then again, it's only humans' blood that has been spilt thus far and Orion isn't supposed to watch over us.

The priest's hand is ruthless as his silver blade bites into my forearm. The cut isn't deep, but the sight of my blood dripping into the ceremonial chalice suddenly makes me queasy. What a start to the trials that would be, if I were to pass out right on the dais from the sight of my own blood.

Breath, wildcat. Tavias's voice sounds inside my head. *It will be over soon.*

I startle and look over at him just as the priest starts his questioning about our desire to seek Orion's leave to enter the trials. Tavias's attention remains on the priest but I can hear him chuckle tightly inside my head. *Yes, you are that easy to read.* The humor fades. *Brace yourself. Don't call out if you can help it.*

Right. Because weakness will make me a target. I swallow as the priest asks the final question, but my voice is steady alongside the males. I don't regret the choice I've made to be here, but that doesn't mean I'm not terrified as I watch the priest's bloody knife draw a glowing symbol in the air. I wrap my hands in my dress to keep them from going to my neck when—

Searing pain consumes my body, making my back arch. I want to scream but I've no breath. Fire and magic carve into me, deep and hot and unrelenting. The world blinks.

Breath, wildcat. Stay with me. Tavias's words sound in my mind, piercing through the agony. However angry he is over being manipulated, there is nothing but concern and steadiness in the connection now. A lifeline for me to hold. *It's just the magic. Stay with me.*

He says it over and over, though he must hurt as much as I do. I wonder if Tavias knows how perilously close to passing out I am. I think Quinton does, because I feel a desperate tug on that bond between us, keeping me in the now.

Several agonizing heartbeats pass before the pain fades away to something dull and deep, and I hear the priest's voice bidding us to rise. Just as I find my feet though, I hear a murmur rushing over the crowd. Tavias turns to me and pales, the priest utters a prayer on my other side.

"What is it?" I ask, my hand going to my neck.

"She's been rejected!" someone calls, others picking up the words and echoing them to each other.

"There is no mark."

"The Goddess Orion has rejected the heir apparent's bride!" Geoffrey shouts above the rest. "All praise the Goddess Orion."

The priest grabs my chin roughly, lifting it high to expose my neck. "There is no mark," he confirms.

"But I felt it," I whisper. "I *felt* the fire and the magic. It has to be there."

"Your human has been tested and found wanting, Tavias," Geoffrey calls again. "Collect up your trash and clear the dais for the real competitors."

"I don't understand," I say, grabbing Tavias's forearm before he can indeed lead me off the dais. Desperation washes over me. "I felt the burn. The pain. I swear."

"Stop." Quinton's cold quiet certainty makes even the priest flinch. "She is marked."

The priest sighs and takes my chin again. "She—"

Quinton's growl is so full of violence that the priest releases me at once and backs away. Stepping up behind me, Quinton rips the back of my dress down the center, the material giving beneath the shearing force.

"Goddess Orion," the priest whispers under his breath.

Taking my shoulders, Quinton twists my bared back toward the crowd. "The goddess *has* bestowed a mark on her," he announces. "A Dragon's mark. Do you not agree, High Priest?"

The priest's nostrils flare, a vein standing out and pulsing beneath his tattooed skin. He looks ready to spit nails.

"Acknowledge the mark," Tavias demands, magic playing over his scales as he steps up beside Quinton. Tavias's previously clear back now bears an intricate design of dragon's wings, the same ones that I see on Cyril and Hauck and Quinton. Is that what's on my back now too? The tattoo is beautiful and large enough to leave almost no patch of skin without color. No wonder it hurt so greatly to receive. Tavias raises his voice, pitching it across the ballroom as if commanding a battlefield. "Orion has accepted our pack and our bride, Kitterny. Acknowledge her, High Priest, or suffer the force of Orion's wrath."

"The mark is acknowledged," the priest admits, though the glare he gives me is nothing but utter hatred. As if I'd offended him personally.

"It seems the goddess isn't the only one to have marked this human." A voice that sounds like Ettienne but isn't him suddenly calls, with more than a little amusement. Salazar. I recognize him from when Autumn pointed him out. Standing close to the dais, Salazar now extends a crackle of his magic to flick against the top of my breast, where my dress has slipped down just enough to make Quinton's bite mark visible.

Shit. I pull my ripped dress back up hastily, but that only makes everything worse.

"My congratulations to you, brother," Salazar turns to Ettienne, whose face is flashing a dark shade of burgundy. "One of your pups has taken a mate, it seems. May their union be joyous and long."

A union between a fae and a mortal, especially one bound for the Equinox Trials, would be anything but long.

"Interesting choice," Geoffrey drawls. "Were all the sheep taken?"

A few choking laughs turn into all out roars of laughter until the whole ballroom is so full of catcalls that the priests

78

have to sound the gongs just to get the ceremony back on track. Devastation fills me like thick molasses as I see the humiliation now etching Ettienne's features and Quinton's hard resolve as he steps in front of me, shielding me from the crowd.

What in stars' name did you two do? Tavias's voice whispers in my mind and, for the first time, I hear genuine fear in it. If just a show of concern was too great a weakness to let be known, how much more dangerous was a public mating bond?

CHAPTER 9

Cyril

*C*yril's mind was a storms' blasted mess. Pacing the length of the small preparation chamber to which they'd been escorted to at the end of the pledge ceremony, Cyril felt like his skin was too tight around him. The sensation that he was looking too long, too wrong, too *something* at Kit—at Quinton's mate—was burning him inside. Had been ever since the mated pair had walked into the pledge ball and turned everything on its head.

Cyril had been struggling to breathe since Kitterny left. Now that she was back though, breathing was harder still—if for an utterly different reason. All it took was for Kit to move an eyebrow, or make one of those little hand motions to shift a strand of hair or pull up the ripped gown she was still clutching closed, and Cyril was ready to throw her atop the nearest table and feast on her right then and there.

At which point, Cyril's scent on her would be enough to drive Quinton to murder—if Kitterny didn't beat him to it and jab a dagger into Cyril's eye. The fury rolling off her now was certainly a match to Tavias's usual temper.

"Where is Quinton?" Kit demanded for the second time. She glared around, as if to reassure herself that her mate wasn't hiding in the attached bathing chamber or under the food-laden table the servants had prepared for them as a sendoff feast. Zeroing in on Cyril, she braced her fists against her hips. "Why did Ettienne hold Quinton back?"

Cyril stiffened, not sure what to say. Ettienne held Quinton back to punish him. Publicly most likely. He could do little else given the public humiliation for the way the mating bond was revealed. The deception of Kit's return was at least a private matter, but the way the news of the bond had come out? No king could let it slide. And Ettienne was in a precarious position as it was with Salazar nipping on his heels.

At least Ettienne thought that punishing Quinton alone would suffice. Dragons healed faster than humans, and if he'd gone after Kit as well… Cyril didn't want to think of what would have happened then.

"Quinton will be back." Tavias fired back at her. Now that they were in private, Tavias was all but punching the walls, the lightning playing along his scales sending off sparks.

"What isn't—"

"We are all needed for the trials, so he has to be, doesn't he?" Tavias growled, cutting off Kit's protest. Shoving the table out of his way, he stalked toward her. "Meanwhile, how about you explain why you two decided to wage a campaign on sanity behind our backs?"

Hauck caught the table's edge, steadying it before it tipped over.

Kit, meanwhile, turned to face Tavias. The deliberate slowness of her motions set off alarm bells in Cyril's head. The timid slave girl who they'd once hoarded from a human estate had been long gone, but this version of Kitterny, the one willing to go toe to toe with the fiercest of dragons, used to be harder to bring out. Now though, she shone in all her glory and Cyril could not be more proud. Even if he knew that nothing about the next few moments would be pleasant.

Hauck was already surreptitiously putting himself in front of the table, lest things came to blows and they lost the food they'd be wise to take with them. It was never a good sign when *Hauck* was the one keeping things from getting worse.

"It's good to see you again too, Tavias," Kit told the heir apparent to the Massa'eve throne. Her voice sliced like a knife through the room. With her dress torn, the tattoo of dragon's wings made it a force of will to look anywhere but her bared skin. Cyril pressed his hand against the wall to fight the urge to trace his fingers along those lines of ink, to come close and drink in Kit's scent. He had no notion how Tavias could withstand it either, but the pack leader seemed to be holding on to his fury for dear life. Kit's chin rose. "How have you been?"

"How have I been? That's what you have to say for yourself after watching two humans die just during the ceremony?" Of the thirty four packs that started the night, they were down to thirty two—Bianca having taken down one woman, and Orion's mark killing another. "What in blight's hell are you doing back here?"

"You are the one who hoarded me," Kit snapped right back at him. "Or have you forgotten that part?"

Tavias's scales rose like hackles. "I hadn't realized I was hoarding a fool!"

"We made a deal." Kit bared her teeth, no longer bothering to keep hold of her dress. It slid down just enough to leave her neck and shoulders bare, which was nearly enough to make Cyril dizzy. His cock gave a pulsating squeeze that made him see stars from the pressure. "I pledged to help win the Equinox Trials, and so here I am. I apologize if you liked your other human better."

Stars, is that what she thought? That the pack *wanted* Fionna?

"We didn't like Fionna better," said Cyril, though staying out of the fray would have been the wiser path. Still, if they were going to fight, Cyril at least wanted the facts known. "We liked the fact of you staying alive more."

A strange look brushed over Kit's face, but disappeared too quickly for Cyril to read. She twisted toward him, the full power of her fury now directed into his chest.

Tavias let out a long breath.

"What about what I like, Cyril?" Kit demanded.

"So far as I was aware, you also liked you being alive," Cyril said. "Has that changed?"

Ignoring that, Kit stepped toward Cyril and jabbed her finger into his chest. "Did you or did you not tell me that most fae here would enslave the human realm if given the chance?"

"Yes," Cyril said slowly.

"And that Ettienne's hold on the throne is the only defense the human realm has from becoming the fae's personal slave pen? Did you tell me that?"

"I did."

Kit's upper lip pulled back into a snarl as she threw Cyril's own words back at him. "So you tell me then, *has that changed?*"

The heartbeat of silence that followed Kit's demand rang like the priests' gong through Cyril's body, the others in the room all freezing as well. Even Tavias.

Stars. Tavias's mental curse echoed Cyril's own thoughts.

Shame, acidic burning shame, spread slowly through Cyril's chest. The human realm. With everything going on, he'd barely considered the effects of Massa'eve's political strife on it. Sure, he'd discussed the politics of it all during the weeks they spent sailing on the Phoenix, but he'd thought it had all been just that—a discussion of politics. He never thought Kit would take the words as a call to action and responsibility. She'd been a mistreated human slave after all.

Her obligation to her kind was non-existent in the eyes of law or custom or justice. She owed the humans nothing.

But this was Kitterny. The human who'd pulled a spike from a dragon's hide, ignoring the biting jaws and equally biting orders from dragon princes, all because she thought it was the right thing to do. And then, when Cyril took her to task for it, she thrust the rope into his hand. Taking the punishment rather than backing down.

Cyril had been a fool to underestimate her. They'd all been fools.

Of course Kitterny would fight for the humans, when she didn't have to. Because she was Kit. Because she was better than the rest of them.

The four of them—the bloody dragon princes of Massa'eve—were entering the Equinox Trials from simple necessity. Because it was expected of the dragon princes, because Ettienne had made any alternative impossible, because they couldn't find a way out. Meanwhile, Kit—who had every reason in the world to worry about nothing beyond her own hide—she had risen beyond that. She saw the map of the future she wanted and seized it.

Cyril's scales pressed tight against his body, the weight of shame pressing on his shoulders. At the ceremony, he'd dismissed Geoffrey's taunt, but now the words stung anew. Cyril had failed again. That his brothers had failed alongside him, didn't make the situation better.

The pack didn't deserve Kit. Cyril knew it at that moment. Just as he knew that Tavias and Hauck were coming to the same realization, for their scales too were tucking in tight, their heads lowering in mute disgrace.

Kit looked from one male to another, her face hard. "Well?" she demanded. "Has that changed? Are humans no longer in danger from what Salazar's ascending the throne would bring?"

"No," Cyril said quietly. "It hasn't."

"You just didn't think the humans' plight was something I should bother with then, is that it?" She flinched at her own words and shook her head.

"Kit," Cyril started to say then stopped, unable to find the words. There really were none. His chest squeezed, the shame burning its way through his flesh more fiercely than the mark had. Though it was too little too late, Cyril dropped to his knees instead, his head bowed and tilted slightly to the side to expose the vulnerable part of his neck to Kit.

Cyril heard rather than saw Tavias do the same a few paces away, Hauck following suit a heartbeat later. None of them spoke. There was nothing to say.

"What are you doing?" Kit demanded. Her breaths were still quick and Cyril could hear the too rapid beat of her heart.

"Groveling, by the looks of it." The answer came from Ettienne, the king having opened the door without knocking and strode inside. Quinton walked stiffly behind their father, covertly touching the wall for balance.

Cyril drew in a short breath but didn't move.

Ettienne cleared his throat. "We are short on time. I'd appreciate it if you let them rise."

Kit made a surprised sound in the back of her throat. Though Cyril's gaze remained on the floor, he could clearly imagine the naïve confusion that colored her face just then.

"You are their king, your majesty," Kit said with a small stutter. "I imagine it's your command they await."

"That's because you've more common sense than the lot of them put together," Ettienne said curtly. "But I assure you, my offspring are currently begging your forgiveness for reasons I will not begin to try and fathom, but will accept for reasons of expediency. If you would not mind, Kitterny."

"Um, get up, please," Kit said.

Cyril rose from his knees, taking a careful step back from Kit. He could smell the blood on Quinton and caught the wet patches on the back of his brother's black shirt before the male turned his back to the wall. Quinton was in pain and had been separated from his new mate. Cyril knew better than to stand too close to Kit just now.

Kit studied Quinton for several heartbeats, then twisted to Ettienne. "What did you do to him?" She demanded with a great deal less concern for her continued existence than Cyril wished she had.

"The least that he deserved," Ettienne replied with no trace of remorse. "And the least that I could." Ignoring the furious flare of Kit's nostrils, Ettienne surveyed the entire pack. Despite his schooled face, Ettienne looked more worried than Cyril ever remembered seeing his father.

"I cannot stay more than a few moments," Ettienne said with his usual expedience. "From the logistics, I suspect the carriages transporting the packs to the trial grounds will be here in two hours. Take all the food that will keep with you— the more time you are forced to hunt, the more exposed your human is. Food at the trials will be unpredictable. Feast and famine. I've little more to offer since the trials change every year, but expect to be separated at least once. Do not let your guard down, and do not let Geoffrey provoke you into a fight you are not ready to have. The mating bond," Ettienne's lips tighten for a moment but he doesn't bother glaring at Quinton, "is common knowledge now. It will be used against you. Be prepared."

"How?" Kit asked. "Beyond the whole *caring is a sign of weakness*, how is it actually a material matter?"

Cyril glowered at Quinton, who'd clearly not bothered to explain the basics.

Hauck cleared his throat. "You see—"

"Last time I saw you, Hauck was half way up your skirt at the dinner table," Ettienne told Kit frankly. "Do you know why he keeps away now?"

"Because he's a prick?"

Hauck chortled.

Ettienne did not. "Because he knows that his scent on you might send Quinton into a murderous frenzy."

Kit's eyes and mouth widened together. "Oh."

"As I said," Ettienne said. "You all should figure that part out before there is no one left in the pack for Geoffrey to kill." He pulled a small satchel from his pocket and thrust it into Kit's hands. "There is a vial of Dragon Tears in here. Tend to the shadow before you head out."

With a final glower, Ettienne turned on his heel and strode out of the room, leaving a heavy silence in his wake. No one moved. No one dared to even breathe too deeply. No one except Kit.

"Is he right?" she demanded of Quinton. "Are you going to lose your rutting mind when I go too near them?"

Quinton swallowed. "I don't know."

A bell chimed, making Cyril acutely aware of the time.

Kit drew a long breath and let it out. "One way to find out." Before anyone could stop her, Kit strode up to Hauck and pressed her mouth over his.

CHAPTER 10

Quinton

Quinton had been prepared. Both the punishment he'd known would be coming, and for this moment, when his mate would touch his brothers with the kind of desire that she reserved for them alone. He'd known both would be hard to endure, and he'd steeled himself for the pain. He'd been prepared.

At least he thought he had.

Now, seeing Kit's mouth cover Hauck's with the kind of passion she would never have for Quinton, he was realizing how short his preparations had fallen. His bond with Kit had been forced. The pull to rut she'd felt afterwards was all but involuntary. She'd touched Quinton because magic made her do so. But Hauck, Kit kissed him because she wanted to.

And it hurt. So much so that the physical pain of his lashed back felt like a lifeline.

Yet, Quinton couldn't look away either. His cock gave a pulsating squeeze as Kit's mouth covered Hauck's, her fingers sliding with sinful delight through his mop of red hair before trailing along his scales.

Hauck let out a moan of approval, the scales shifting to indulgent emerald hues beneath Kit's touch.

Kit deepened her kiss. Her ripped dress had slipped several inches down her shoulders, allowing Hauck's fingers full access to her tattooed back. Hauck took the invitation, trailing his calloused fingers along the column of Kit's spine.

Quinton knew exactly how that smooth soft skin felt, and the fact that it wasn't *his* hand brushing Kit's body… it was hard.

Quinton swayed slightly, moving his feet farther apart to keep his balance. He'd expected to be angry. Furious on a primal level. Ready to rip Hauck and the others limb from limb for looking—much less touching—his mate. He knew beyond a shadow of a doubt that if it had been any male other than his brother touching Kit, that male would not draw his next breath. But with Hauck there, Quinton felt different.

Desperate to join. Aroused. Envious.

Coming up from behind Kit, Tavias ran his palms over her curves. She moaned with pleasure, arching herself back against his obvious hardness, even as her mouth remained on Hauck's. Tavias grunted in approval and buried his nose in Kit's thick hair, making Quinton too aware of her cinnamon and citrus scent even from across the room.

"You've not tried to rip anyone's limbs off yet," Cyril said from beside him. The dragon had his sword out but pointed to the floor, his body bladed between Quinton and the sensual reunion playing itself out just paces away. A wise precaution, through unnecessary. Even if Quinton wanted to attack, he was in no shape to do so with any effectiveness. Maybe that too was part of Ettienne's plan.

Kit made another sound of pleasure and Quinton's cock jerked again, making him see stars from the building pressure. Both in his cock and in his soul.

"Quinton?" Cyril was speaking again. Possibly had been for a while. "Quinton look at me."

There was a note of primal command in the order, and Quinton turned to Cyril obediently.

Cyril had sheathed his sword, his face concerned. "What's going on inside your head?"

"Nothing."

"I'd expected you to at least destroy the room by now," Cyril pointed out, each word digging deeper into Quinton's shields. It was annoying as fuck and Quinton didn't bother to respond.

Cyril clicked his tongue. "That you aren't even trying -"

"Oh for fuck's sake," Quinton snapped finally. "She likes it. Alright? Is that what you want to hear? She likes it. You'd have to be bloody blind not to see it." The words came through gritted teeth. "If I hurt them, I hurt her."

And wasn't that the ironic truth? For as much as the mating bond roared its jealousy, it also made it impossible for Quinton to stop what was happening. How could he attack Hauck, when he was making every fiber of Kit's body sing with pleasure and trust and a hundred other things that she deserved? How could he rip out Tavias's jugular, when his scent made shivers of desire rush over Kit's skin? The mating bond served up all the truths to Quinton, stripping him of his defenses one at a time. Kit had missed Hauck's teasing heat. Missed Tavias's dangerous touch. With the mating bond between them, Quinton felt Kit's sensations as vividly as his own just then.

Quinton's hand curled into a fist, his nails digging into his palm. He focused on the sensation. On his breath. On watching each of Kit's breaths. The way her lashes fluttered when she shut her eyes. How she made this tiny involuntary sound each time a tendril of pleasure caressed her.

Everything.

"You know, I used to think that she was the weak link," Cyril said after a few moments of blessed quiet. "A fragile human who couldn't ride or fight or keep herself out of harm's way."

"She still can't. Especially the latter." The riding and fighting had improved.

Cyril snorted. "Most certainly not the latter. But she isn't the weak link, is she?"

"No." Quinton couldn't look away from where Tavias's

hand slipped down Kit's inner thigh, the scent of her arousal now spiking the air.

"We weren't a pack," Cyril's words were softly spoken, as if he'd not been sure whether he wished to voice them aloud. "Not in anything beyond name and custom. Not before her."

"We are what we've been forged to be," said Quinton. He cut himself off, knowing he was stepping into treacherous territory. Cyril was the most powerful of them, his magic poised to eclipse even Ettienne's. But something had happened to lock that power up. Quinton didn't know what it was, only that Cyril came back changed after one fairly minor skirmish had gone awry. Cyril never spoke of what happened exactly and Tavias, who was likely the only person who knew, didn't either.

Yet on the Phoenix, Quinton had glimpsed sparks of that powerful male once more. He had no doubt that too was Kit's doing.

"You should go join them." Cyril pointed his chin at the obvious pulsating hardness in Quinton's britches. "You obviously want to."

Quinton turned his head away.

"Quinton." There was that command in Cyril's voice again.

Quinton growled. "I can't."

"Did Ettienne hurt you beyond —"

He struck his palm against the wall, the last strands of control snapping. "Ettienne has nothing to do with this." Quinton drew a breath, keeping his voice low, though no less harsh. "Don't you rutting get it? She *wants* Hauck and Tavias —and you too, if you decided you trusted me to not lose my shit. What she feels for you, it's real. Me, I'm just instinct. A pull of a bloody bond she never asked for. It's not the same. It never will be."

Cyril's brows pulled together. "What kind of horseshit is that?"

He forced his hand to unfurl. He was a shadow. The shit he'd done in the name of the throne, stars, maybe this was the world's justice. There had to be a reckoning for all the deaths Quinton caused and wasn't this a much more fitting punishment than to be smitten in return? "Can you assist with my wounds?" Quinton asked briskly, motioning to the bathing chamber.

He didn't want Kit seeing his back.

"Of course." Cyril picked up the satchel Kit had put down, the one with the vial of Dragon Tears. The potion was nearly as hard to get as the fertility elixir and it hurt like the fires of the abyss. But it worked like nothing else. Trust Ettienne to have his cake and eat it too—punish Quinton without compromising the pack's chances at the trial.

"Where do you two think you are going?" Kit's voice snagged the pair of them before they could get halfway to the adjoining room. She was tangled so deeply in Hauck's arms that Quinton doubted even a sliver of light could worm between them now. He imagined himself there in Hauck's place, and regretted it immediately since it made his heart pump so hard that it irritated his wounds.

Kit scraped her teeth along her bottom lip. "This is supposed to be the part where we come together."

"You came together," Quinton said. "I didn't kill anyone. Victory. Now I'd like to move on."

Kit pushed away from Hauck and Tavias, striding across the large chamber like a battlefield general. Her gown fluttered behind her, the too long skirts swishing about with each movement. Sometime during her reunion with Hauck and Tavias, her hair had come undone—likely with assistance—and now framed her shoulders in snow white locks. Quinton couldn't decide which he found more distracting, the dyed color or original. Both were magnificent.

"You didn't kill anyone, that's your metric of cooperation?" Stopping a pace away, Kit crossed her arms over her chest. Quinton wasn't sure how someone so small that she had to crane her head back just to look him in the eye could fill the room with her presence, but when it came to Kit nothing made sense. She shook her head. "Stop playing at lone wolf," she ordered. "Or lone dragon. Whatever."

"It's what I am."

"That's what you were." Her eyes flashed.

"I didn't kill anyone," Quinton hissed, his pulse pounding through him. Yes, that should damn well count for something. Everything about the chamber was feeling too small, the walls too tight. His voice rose. "If you imagine anything about watching you -" he cut off, not knowing what to say. His back hurt. His soul ached. It was all he could do to salvage the tatters of himself. "What do you want from me?" he demanded.

Breaching the few feet of distance between them, Kit pressed her hand against Quinton's cheek. She had no idea how much that soft touch made him ache with need. Too much. "Honesty," she said softly.

"She also wants you to stop moving away," Tavias added, coming to stand beside Kit. As if the scent he'd already left on her wasn't enough. A band tightened around Quinton's chest, making it hard to draw breath.

"Honesty?" He grabbed Kit's wrist harder than he'd intended and she winced. A small movement but it was the last strain Quinton could weather. Everything inside him exploded. "You want honesty? Here is honesty." The words came in a harsh burst, clouded by pain and need and fraying self-control. "What you want, what you deserve, is a pack. And I'm not pack. Not this one, not any one. I'm a shadow. That is all I am and will ever be."

Quinton did not realize the truth—and sting—of those words until he shouted them into Kit's face. His hands clenched and unclenched at his sides looking for purchase that wasn't there. "If you don't trust your own eyes and instincts, then trust theirs." He jerked his head toward Tavias. "Do you know why I had to keep your coming to the pledge ball a secret? Because I knew that a real pack would not allow its heart to be served up on a silver platter for scavengers to hunt. Dragons protect their mates. But that's not what I did. So let's all call the truths as they are. I'm darkness and ruthlessness. I'm the shadow that takes lives in the night. And yes, maybe I deserve to watch you savor my brothers' touch, knowing that you only tolerate mine from instinct—but that's one punishment that's too harsh for me to bear. So I'm not. I'm turning away like a coward."

A tremor ran through him, drops of blood from his back splattering on the white marble floor. He drew a ragged breath, meeting Kit's wide eyes. "You are the one bright light I've ever had in my dark existence. You don't think I know that I don't deserve you? That what I did, mating with you, bringing you here, might extinguish it once and for all? I do many things human, but there is one that I do not—I don't lie to myself."

Quinton clamped his mouth shut, his panting breath the only sound in the room that had suddenly gone preternaturally silent. He felt the weight of everyone's stares burning through him like fire arrows and opened his shoulders to accept them all. One after another, after another. He... he hadn't meant to say any of that. Not aloud. But Kit had asked for the truth and he... Blight take him. For the first time in his life Quinton did not know how to fight.

He took a step back.

Kit took a step forward.

Quinton stopped.

She did as well. She didn't speak. Instead, her fingers went to the buttons of the shirt he had so painstakingly put back on before returning. The first. Second. Third. The shirt opened to his sternum, the air touching his skin. He didn't know what Kit thought she was doing, but he desperately hoped she wasn't going to try to get the thing off of him.

It would hurt too much in too many different ways. Yet he was powerless to stop her.

"What are you doing?" Quinton asked when Kit thankfully stopped with the buttons.

"Looking for the right spot." She ran her fingers over his neck, right where it met his shoulder. The jolt of sensation speared down his spine.

"For?" Quinton ground out.

The tip of her finger stopped right over Quinton's pounding pulse. He could feel his skin pressing against her touch with every beat of his heart. If she were to plunge a dagger there, he'd bleed out in minutes. But blight take him, he wouldn't fight her if she did.

He tilted his head a fraction, exposing more of his vulnerable neck. If Kit wanted his life for bringing her into this mess, then she had it.

"You are too tall," she said after a moment. "I need you to kneel."

Quinton did, dropping to his knees before her without hesitation.

"Thank you," Kit said softly. And then she braced one hand on the back of his neck and bit him.

Quinton jerked, the tiny sting blossoming on his neck demanding his singular focus. His hands gripped Kit's hips involuntarily, though he was unsure whose balance he was trying to save. When she pulled back though, his blood red on her lips, he knew it was his own need for stability that kept him from moving.

"I claim you as my mate, Quinton of Massa'eve," Kit said, her palm over his cheek. "My bite might not have dragon magic the way yours does, but you've enough for us both on that front. So there we go. No more of this one sided *I dragged you into this* horseshit."

"But I *did -*"

"You bound us. And I brought us here. I think we are even. And if you don't like lying to yourself, then you should practice saying a new truth: you aren't a lone shadow anymore. You are bonded. Mated. Tied to me. You can like it or not. That's your choice. But being alone? That's done."

Kit's words rang over the room, sinking into Quinton's bones. Still on his knees, he pressed his forehead into Kit's shoulder. He had no words, not for the powerful sensation echoing through him. Kit was wrong about not having magic. She had power. A kind that could slay a dragon right where he knelt.

There was movement behind him and the tussling of clothes and bodies as Tavias cut the back of Quinton's shirt and Cyril pulled out the vial of Dragon Tears. Hauck, who'd managed to fetch a pitcher of water and a wash bowl in the last few minutes, dabbed a washcloth at the top of Quinton's shoulder and growled in soft disapproval.

None of it was odd in isolation exactly, but taken together, it felt an awful lot like his brothers were fussing.

Quinton lifted his head from Kit's shoulder. "What are

the three of you doing?" He was asking a damn lot of that lately. He tried to pull away, but Tavias seemed to have anticipated the move and gripped Quinton's shoulder firmly.

"What we should have been doing all along," Tavias said curtly, though the strange shame coating his words was impossible to miss. "Every time you came back from training too stiff to move easily. And every time you come back from another assignment with that silence of yours darkening your eyes."

"Being a shadow is your job, Quinton," Cyril said. "Being our brother, our pack, that's what you are."

"And being my mate. You are that too," Kit added. "So deal with it."

Cyril opened the vial, releasing an acrid scent into the air. "Unfortunately, this will hurt. Take some deep breaths."

Quinton did take some deep breaths—he needed them to get on his feet and out of this... whatever this was.

"Oh no you don't." Kit's voice was soft, but it was a clear order if Quinton had ever heard one. Her hand pressed against his cheek, keeping him in place. "You aren't going to fight."

Before Quinton could object—or even clarify what he wasn't to fight, Kit brushed her lips over his mouth. The feel of her soft mouth made Quinton jerk forward for reasons that had nothing to do with the droplets of Dragon Tears that Cyril started to dribble onto his back.

It was like being on fire, from both the outside and inside. Kit tangled her fingers in his hair. He knew she was trying to distract him from the pain, and *ruuuuut*, it was working. He suddenly couldn't care less if the whole of Massa'eve's western legion wanted to pour magic-infused acid on his wounds, so long as he could get drunk on his mate in the process.

"You are mine, Shadow," Kit murmured against Quinton's mouth as he savored her taste with every stroke of their tongues. "And I'm yours. And the pack's. We are each other's."

For the first time in centuries, Quinton's mind went silent.

His brothers were just getting the final bandages into place—Quinton, still drunk on his mate and his pain swaying slightly—when the door to the chamber opened.

"Your Highnesses," the entering servant kept his gaze on the floor as he deposited a stack of what looked like gray and purple uniforms onto a chair. "I am to tell you that it's Orion's will to depart earlier than intended. You are to leave now."

CHAPTER 11

Kit

*D*espite the windowless carriage in which we travel, I feel the moment we cross into the trial grounds, the rune on my back coming alive with a sensation akin to a dozen stinging bees. It only lasts a few moments, but it's enough to make Quinton grip the edge of the bench. The potion Ettienne had provided knitted his flesh together with ruthless efficiency, but there had been too much damage for even it to fully erase the marks from Quinton's back.

I want to put my hand over his thigh and remind him that he isn't alone. Not anymore. Maybe it's silly to think that my touch might give him relief, but I long to try anyway.

"Stop it." Quinton half growls in my direction.

"Stop what?"

"Stop looking at me like you are contemplating a hug." He makes the word sound like an attack. No, not an attack. He'd find a random assault less objectionable.

"I had zero intention of hugging you," I assure him. It's not even a lie. The thought of squeezing him with his back half flayed open was never a consideration.

He gives me a suspicious glare and goes about checking his weapons. We only have what we'd brought to the pledge ball, but Quinton is always armed. He pulls a knife out of his boot and hands it to me.

The blade is light and has a rose engraved on the hilt.

Hauck must spot the engraving the same time I do, because he snaps the weapon from my hand for closer examination. "Is this your version of giving a girl flowers?"

Quinton grabs the knife back from Hauck and thrusts it back into my hands. "Why in blights' path would I give her flowers?" he asks defensively. "What would she even do with them?"

"My mistake," Hauck says too innocently. We've been traveling in a carriage for over six hours and he is plainly looking for entertainment. "You must have gotten a flower engraved blade for yourself."

Quinton bristles. I know him well enough to notice that the pain and stress has frayed the edges of his usual self-control—a fact that Hauck is plainly aware of and enjoying. Quinton's jaw tightens. "It's not my bloody knife. I retrieved it from Bianca's target."

"You are giving me a present you literally pulled out of a corpse?" I clarify. Hauck is right. This is fun. Especially after six hours of utter bouncing boredom. Honestly, I don't even feel bad.

The tops of Quinton's ears—and scales—turn pink. "It's not a present."

"That's the part of the sentence you found objectionable?"

His nostrils flare. "It's a weapon. And it's decent. So yes, I took it for you. What's wrong with—"

"Oh for stars' sake. Can you two stop toying with a shadow?" Cyril gives me and Hauck a reproachful look.

Hauck lifts his hands, palm up in indignant innocence. "What did *I* do?"

Shaking his head, Cyril finishes spoiling our fun by handing me an apple from the makeshift pack we'd turned the tablecloth into. "Eat."

"I'm alright." I don't know when food will be available, and don't want to take from our provisions. My stomach growls.

Eat, Tavias orders, directly into my mind. He puts a bit of bite behind the order, making it echo inside my skull.

Deciding against arguing, I eat the apple—core included. I am hungry. But also, the males are watching every bite as if afraid I'll starve to death in the next five minutes. Their protectiveness has kicked in with a vengeance, and I'm going to need to pick my battles over the next few days.

Irritating Quinton had been decidedly more amusing.

Despite all the looming terror of the trials, I can't help

being curious about how it would all work. So far as I can tell, the priests of Orion wield a different kind of magic than any of the fae, dragon shifter or not. I guess they must, if they are to be entrusted with keeping the precious elixir and remaining neutral in the dragons' political affairs.

It is another hour before we come to a full stop and the driver opens the doors. Cyril and Tavias hold me back, not letting me out of the carriage until after Quinton and Hauck step out first, look around and give their nods of approval. The pair then flanks me when I finally exit onto a meadow encircled by dozens of carriages.

The trial grounds are surprisingly beautiful. The nippy air kissing my face is ruffling a carpet of violet irises and golden daffodils that pepper the lush grass. Ahead of us, the riot of unblemished color stretches toward the mountainous forest flanking the field. Great oaks with twisted limbs and gnarled bark watch us like weathered warriors. Farther up the slope, towering firs and pines silhouette the sky with their needle-clad limbs.

On the east side of the field, a massive structure crafted from polished black stone spirals toward the clear blue sky. Sparkling glass worked into its facade catches the light just right, glowing even in the morning hours. It takes me a moment to realize that the reflective orbs aren't random, but mirror the constellations. A tribute to the Goddess Orion, if there ever was one. This must be the citadel that Ettienne spoke about.

"I've never seen anything like this," I tell Cyril, who is closest to me.

"Nor have I." Given that his attention is fixed firmly on the other competitors exiting their carriages, I don't think we are talking about the same thing. In fact, all the males in my pack are on alert, scanning each new face as if waiting for one of them to break the semi-circular formation and launch an attack.

I wonder how many of the males here the princes know. We'd been given uniforms to change into, gray trousers and loose tunics, trimmed with a dazzling purple the color of Tavias's amethyst scales. The other packs are dressed the same, save for the trim color, which I think matches the scales of the pack leader.

Geoffrey's pack is a few groups to the right of us. Their trim is black.

Of the thirty two packs who are now with us on the trial grounds, about half seem to have brought anything along. Some used the tablecloth like we did, others having taken off their tunics to create makeshift bundles. I wonder how many of those standing on the colorful meadow with us will be dead soon.

The priest from the pledge ball strolls to the middle of the field, crushing the flowers beneath his boots. He draws a small mark in the air.

"Competitors, welcome to the trial grounds." Whatever magic that was, it's amplifying his voice to an all-encompassing boom.

"Nice trick," I murmured to Tavais. "Can you do that too?"

No. Pay attention.

"You have all felt your passage through the barrier, which is several miles in all directions from the citadel. You will find visual markers around the perimeter of the grounds to remind you of the boundaries. Should any of the dragons pass beyond the boundary, your mark will dissolve and you will be physically unable to re-enter. Your pack may continue the competition without you. Should any of the humans pass beyond the boundary, the mark will end their life."

A hand settles on the nape of my neck. Hauck. I'm not sure which of us he is trying to reassure, but I'm grateful for it.

"Your first trial will start tomorrow," the priest continues. "You will hear three bells half an hour prior. When you do, proceed to the competition arena inside the citadel. Two bells will sound at the fifteen minute mark, and one when one minute remains. Anyone who is not at the arena at the trial's start will be disqualified and escorted beyond the edge of the trial grounds."

Which for the humans among us means death. Right.

"You may camp wherever you wish until then. Know that the citadel itself is sacred ground. Anyone attempting to harm another competitor outside the arena within the citadel, will be disqualified."

I notice that he says nothing about harming each other outside the citadel itself.

We take high ground, Tavias's voice sounds in my head. I'm pretty certain he is talking to Cyril and wonder if he knows I can hear him. *As high as we can get with a thirty minute response.*

"The first three wagons in the caravan hold supplies you may find useful," the priest continues benevolently. "Each pack may send one representative to the supply wagons to collect whatever they'd like. The Goddess Orion wishes good fortune to all."

A gong sounds somewhere, marking the end of the high priest's speech. At once, there is a palpable charge in the air as all the dragons glare at each other.

Quinton starts toward the supply wagons. Even in gray instead of black, he is violence incarnate and I almost feel bad for whoever might try to get in his way.

Hauck bars Quinton's path. A suicidal move if I've ever seen one, but Hauck grins easily and stuffs his hands into his pockets while Quinton glowers murder at him. "Forgetting for a moment that you are still walking with half your hide," Hauck drawls, "can we acknowledge that when it comes to... acquisitions... I'm the one with experience?"

"Stars know I can vouch for that," Cyril mutters under his breath. "And for the number of times I've wanted to flay you alive for that talent."

Hauck flashes a grin, his thick lashes turning up. "I knew you'd come around to appreciate me one day."

Quinton sighs dramatically, but yields and Hauck struts away to acquire provisions.

The four of us turn toward the mountains but make it less than a dozen steps before Geoffrey and his pack block our path. They are all large and good looking, but there is a cruelty around the corners of their mouths that reminds me of some of the nobles at Agam estate. Ones who thought they were owed whatever they wished, especially by slaves.

Tavias lifts his chin, his scales pressed tight against his temples. "Move."

Geoffrey tucks his thumbs into his belt. "Come, cousin. That is no way to start an alliance."

"An alliance?" Tavias echoes with the incredulity that I feel rippling through the rest of the pack. "With you?"

Geoffrey shrugs. "With who else? Not a permanent one, of course. Just until our packs are the only ones left. We both know that the elixir must remain within the royal blood one way or another, and that means either your pack or mine. Whatever else, we must think of Massa'eve first and foremost."

"That we do." Tavias rolls his shoulders, as if trying to work the kinks out after the ride. "But, I think there has been a misunderstanding."

"How so?"

"I'd rather see the elixir poured down the latrine than watch you procreate," Tavias replies with a nonchalance that makes me fight back a laugh. "In fact, I might go so far as to ensure I personally cut off your balls to prevent such a disaster from befalling the realm. I must think of Massa'eve first and foremost, you understand."

A slow smile spreads over Geoffrey's mouth. "I am going to remember you said that."

"I'll take pleasure in knowing I live in your brain rent free." Tavias continues forward, shouldering Geoffrey out of the way to clear the path.

"I am curious about something, though." Geoffrey's drawl hits my back just when I think we are past his blockade. "With the bond and all, what will Quinton feel when I take his human cunt for a ride?"

Quinton stops, going preternaturally still. Anger that's not my own hits me, making it difficult to think.

"Would it feel like it's him being fucked?" Geoffrey wonders aloud, his grin widening when we turn back toward him. He looks at Quinton directly now. "I'll take her ass first, just so it feels familiar. As a courtesy. But then—"

Quinton snarls and lunges forward, Tavias and Cyril intersecting him a pace away from Geoffrey.

Not now, Tavias orders with his mind.

My chest tightens. Not now, because now Quinton is still weak and we are without Hauck, who went to get supplies. Not now, because we are in the middle of a stars' damned meadow where anyone else might join in. How many here have a bone to pick with the crown? Even though no one is close enough to hear our exchange, I know the others are watching. Hell, Geoffrey probably planned it this way.

"Maybe I'm looking at this all wrong," Geoffrey amends,

speaking louder now. Playing to the audience that's slowly gathering. "It takes a certain type of bravery to bring a mate to a place like this, after all. Knowing what will be done to her here. Tell me, Shadow, is this part of your training perhaps? Something your father is having you do? The way Ettienne treats our lands, I would not be surprised at all."

"Shut your mouth," Tavias says, stepping up to Quinton's shoulder.

Ettienne's warning returns to me. The one about me being a weakness that would be exploited. Geoffrey knows exactly what buttons to push.

"We should go," I tell the males. "Find a good camping spot. High ground or whatever."

"High ground or whatever?" Geoffrey echoes. More packs are around us now, sizing us up. "Is it the human giving orders in this pack, then? The wench has put a leash and muzzle on the princes of Massa'eve it seems. Is this what we all have to look forward to if you lot keep the throne?"

"I said, shut your mouth." Lightning dances along Tavias's raised scales. That's two of us whose skin Geoffrey has gotten under in as many minutes.

"It's not my mouth you should be worrying about, pack leader," Geoffrey replies, sneering toward Quinton. "What do you imagine will happen the first time Lady Kitterny's mouth screams and begs? What will happen to your little pack then? Will you even be able to control your own?"

Geoffrey points toward Quinton, who really does seem more feral beast than cool warrior now. His eyes are narrowed, the pupils compressed to slits, his lips curled above bared teeth.

"I had a dog like that once," Bianca adds in a strangely musical voice. "A decent mutt until he got bit and went rabid. Putting him down was the best thing for him really."

My bond mark flares and I'm suddenly vibrating with the same rage that has Quinton snarling. I don't know where his anger ends and mine begins. I'm not even sure I care. My blood seethes, my vision stained crimson. All I want is to claw Bianca's eyes out.

Three out of four. I know this is wrong, but can't bring myself to care. My hand reaches for the knife nestled against my waist. I imagine sinking the blade into Bianca and the satisfyingly grisly thought fuels my fury even more.

The thunderous drumming of my heart amplifies, the crescendo reverberating through the tether of my bond with Quinton.

"Enough." Cyril's voice cuts through the air, sharp and commanding like a steel blade.

I didn't even see magic start to gather around Cyril, before an invisible blast knocked me flat on my ass. Me, Quinton, Tavias, and all of Geoffrey's pack, we all fall like dominos away from where Cyril stands his ground, his palms extended in either direction.

Power dances around him, something that I feel more than see. His eyes, molten sapphire blue, burn with a ferocity that is both terrifying and mesmerizing. A muscle twitches along his jaw, the only sign of his contained fury. His lips press into a hard line, a final, stern command that brooks no argument.

And there is none. Not from anyone. There is hush passing through the clearing, every eye in the trial grounds fixed on who I realize is the strongest dragon here.

Cyril.

CHAPTER 12

Kit

"That's enough." Cyril enunciates each word. He doesn't shout, yet his voice carries over the clearing with an awesome finality. It's the Cyril I saw on the quarterdeck of the Phoenix, only more so. "We are here to compete and we shall do so in a way that honors the dragon line. All of us."

Several heartbeats of silence answer Cyril's command, as everyone in the meadow gathers themselves together. Geoffrey rises off the ground first, jerking his chin at his pack. They move away without another word. Then we do the same.

The crowd of onlookers parts before Cyril, letting us

pass. His silence bodes no argument or comment from anyone. Not even me.

We are just at the edge of the clearing and about to start onto the mountain path when I pull my wits back around. What happened at the clearing, both with Quinton and me and then with Cyril... we needed to talk about it. Except that if I know anything about the dragons, they'll turn vegetarian before they start a conversation.

I draw breath, ready to ask my first question.

"I'll take the high view," Cyril tells Tavias suddenly. "Give you top cover."

"I can do that," Tavias says, but Cyril is already moving farther away from us. He isn't looking at me. At anyone. There is a flash of light then, and a great blue dragon unfurls its wings in the place where Cyril just stood. The iridescent scales glimmer in the sunlight showing off the dragon's belly as he climbs into the air. The sight is so gorgeous, I can't look away until Tavias nudges me into motion, grumbling about that elusive high ground we need to secure.

Both my burbling thoughts and my relief at a chance to stretch my legs after hours in the carriage keeps my attention for only a little while before my body starts to protest Tavias's pace. He's switched into his military general mode and is searching for an optimal defensive position as if the wellbeing of the whole realm rests on finding just the right stretch of dirt on which to settle our asses.

He wants elevated ground, he explains curtly when I ask. With natural concealment but good outward visibility.

Something with access to water but not in wetlands. A place far enough to be out of the way, but close enough to the citadel to allow quick access. Enough foliage to camouflage us but not so much that the males can't shift.

I stop listening to his explanations as the incline steepens, becoming as much mountain as forest. The smell of damp earth fills my nostrils, a comfort amidst the growing burn in my calves and lungs. My fingers scrape over rough bark as I use a tree for support, the sharp tingle of resin sticking to my skin. I want to ask how we can be hiking for hours to find a place within thirty minutes of the citadel, but I've no breath to spare—nor any real desire to listen to the answer.

Despite his wounds, Quinton moves over the land with ease and Tavias appears not to notice the incline at all. Which is getting irritating. When my foot slips on a patch of wet fern leaves, I let myself go down on one knee instead of trying to regain balance. A sneaky way of clawing a short break for myself without having to ask for one.

Quinton gives me a hand up too quickly for my taste. We are hiking in stars blasted circles. We have to be. Just like the circles the insects buzzing around us are keeping to.

The forest is a riot of green now, the foliage so dense it blots out the sun and dapples the ground in shadow. The light plays tricks on my eyes, the underbrush appearing to shift and move while the towering evergreens hem us in. Sweat pours down my back, my only reprieve coming when small gusts of wind brush my heated skin with their tang of pine and the sharper, slightly acidic note of the towering spruce.

I lick my lips, my mouth dry despite the damp forest air. I really wish for a gulp of water, but that requires canteens, which we don't have. Or at least a pause at one of the creeks.

As we pass a burbling brook I'd really like to wash my face in, Tavias makes an evaluative sound with the back of his throat. "You are at your limit."

He doesn't say it as an insult, but I still bristle. "What are you talking about?" I protest. "I didn't even say anything."

"It's not my first day in the field, wildcat." Tossing the bundle of supplies he carries to Quinton, Tavias hauls me over his shoulder like a sack of potatoes.

"Hey!"

Ignoring my indignant protest, the prince proceeds up the incline, his steps sure and steady despite the rough terrain and my added weight.

"Put me down." I squirm, my new upside-down view of the ground less than inspiring. "I can walk."

"And I can sing," says Tavias. "That doesn't mean that I should."

"It is faster if he carries you," Quinton agrees. Unlike with Tavias, there absolutely is judgment in Quinton's tone. I bet he is remembering our endurance training from the Phoenix —or, more accurately, the lack of said training over the last few weeks.

He looks displeased. With me, or himself, or gravity, I don't know. Probably all of the above.

I hate to admit it, but with Tavias carrying me we do move faster. Still, it's another hour before we find a location Tavias deems appropriate and settles us into place. I'm not sure how Hauck finds us, but he is there within a quarter hour, a pack of supplies over his back. There isn't much talk as we set up camp, with Hauck weaving a shelter together and Quinton dissolving into the woods to hunt for meat, which is probably his idea of a relaxing time.

Cyril remains sentry in the skies until the midday meal is ready. I hear him and Tavias arguing about something in hushed tones after he descends, but both go quiet when I approach. Cyril surveys every inch of me as if I've just come out of battle instead of the woven shelter.

"Should I twirl around for you?" I ask him.

"Not necessary."

"Good, because I wasn't actually going to."

"Hmm." Cyril's shoulders are tense as he moves away from Tavias and settles by the cooking fire. Thanks to Hauck we have a pot, and Tavias taught me how to whittle sticks into spoons. There are no bowls but it's not as if we've not shared more intimate things than a soup pot.

I sit next to Cyril. Whatever is bothering him, he isn't ready to talk about it, but when I brush my hand along his cheek he briefly leans into the touch. Hauck joins us as well, passing a flask of whiskey to Cyril. Trust Hauck to come back from a supply run with whiskey.

"Eat," Cyril tells me. Feeding me seems to be a new theme

with the dragons, and they all watch carefully as I dip my spoon into the shared pot.

The moment the soup touches my lips, the world narrows down to the symphony of flavors. There is the earthy richness of Quinton's freshly hunted venison and touches of root vegetables Hauck foraged from beneath the damp earth. The natural caramelized sweetness of the latter contrasts beautifully with the venison's musky strength. My contribution to the cause, mushrooms that I found in a nearby shaded grove, add another umami edge that unfurls on my tongue. It's as if the forest has leaped into the pot and now dances a tantalizing waltz in my mouth.

Quinton grunts softly. "Can you tone it down?"

"What?" I ask around mouthfuls.

"If I wasn't watching what you are actually doing, I'd think you are finding release with one of these assholes just now."

Hauck snorts.

I make a show of licking my spoon, which makes the front of Quinton's britches twitch. Hauck's chuckling turns into a howl of laughter.

"Is this normal?" I ask. "The way our emotions flow through the mating bond?"

Apparently that was the wrong thing to say because the amusement around the fire dies at once.

"No," Cyril answers with curt frankness. "At least not to the extent that it seems to flow between the two of you."

"Is that bad?" I ask.

Quinton opens his mouth to say something but Cyril cuts him off. "We don't know. No one does. A dragon has never mated with a human as far as any of us know. Either way, I imagine the two of you will have to work out a way to separate your own impulses from those flowing through the bond."

I think of what happened with Geoffrey's taunts earlier and can't disagree. I reach for more soup but before I can scoop it up, the forest shrieks with a distant battle cry that vibrates through my whole body. On its heels, I hear a mesh of snarls and roars, the thunderous clash of bodies and scales that silhouette the horizon for a moment before diving down.

Hauck's hand wraps around mine, stopping me from spilling my soup. "That would be the start of the festivities," he says with absurd lightness.

A savage, guttural howl echoes through the sprawling woods. None of the males look remotely surprised though.

"Packs have started attacking each other," Tavias says, dipping his spoon into the soup. "It's a common strategy. Some want to thin the competition, others will use the attacks to acquire supplies. It will go on through the night I expect."

"Oh good," I mutter.

"This is why securing high ground was important," Tavias explains with way too great an ease. Of course. He's used to leading legions into the blight, so camping in the middle of deadly creatures with murder on their minds is probably his idea of a Tuesday. "Which we did."

"Is Geoffrey likely to come after us?" I ask.

"Tonight?" Tavias shakes his head. "No. It would mean pitting his pack against us directly, and those aren't odds he's comfortable with. He'll want things skewed in his favor first."

As he'd tried to do earlier.

"What if we strike first?" Hauck offers. "Shove his machinations up his ass, and be done with it."

"And would you propose we take Kit along on this crusade, putting her in the middle of a dragon battle?" Tavias inquires. "Or leave with one guard and proceed with only three of us against a pack at full strength in its location of choice?"

Neither of those sounds like a good idea to me.

"Don't forget that Geoffrey cares about us losing as much as he cares about him winning," Tavias adds. "He won't hesitate to sacrifice Bianca if need be."

"Won't that take him out of the running?" I ask.

Cyril's lips press into a thin line before he answers. "Not if he secures another pack's human to replace her."

My gaze darts to the horizon, catching momentary flashes through the verdant veil of trees. An eruption of golden flame here, a streak of iridescent scales there, the gleaming crimson orbs of a dragon's eyes.

"Geoffrey is not taking you." Quinton says. I'd not seen him move, but he is suddenly crouching in front of me, his hand on my chin. "No one is. I won't let them."

The bite mark on my breast flares with heat, as if imprinting Quinton's vow on my flesh.

In the distance, the echoes of the dragon brawl strike another note in their disconcerting symphony. I swallow, unable to look away from Quinton's face. His silver eyes darken, flickering with a flame that makes my breath hitch.

Then he moves closer. An emotion stirs over his face, something potent and raw, something that isn't just the instinctive tug of our bond.

With a languid grace that belies the strength coiled within his frame, he leans forward. His large hand cradles the nape of my neck, tilting my face up to meet his. His thumb brushes against my skin in a feather-light caress that I didn't know him even capable of.

Sparks dance along my spine, taking my breath.

Quinton tips his head to the side, scraping his canines gently over my neck. The tiny prickling sensation shoots through me. My mouth parts, my held breath turning to a gasp.

His lips cover mine then, moving slowly. Carefully. His lips are soft against mine, a stark contrast to the hard planes of his body. He tastes like the forest after a storm, wild and refreshing. An intoxicating blend that sets my senses alight.

It isn't like any other kisses we've shared—the desperate, instinct-fueled kisses that stemmed from our bond, from the primal need of dragons. No, this one is different. It is a slow burn, a gentle exploration that stokes a fire in the pit of my belly.

I brush my tongue against his in answer, my hands bracing on the solid muscles of his shoulders.

In the distance, the dragon skirmishes continue to play out. But to me, they are muffled now, muted by the beating of our intertwined hearts.

CHAPTER 13

Cyril

The morning of the first trial day started with deceptive quiet. The sun was well above the horizon, the bells had yet to sound, and Cyril was escorting Kit to the stream to wash up. She'd always have an escort now. Two, if any of the other packs were around. Not that spending more time beside Kit was any hardship. In fact, it was quite the opposite.

"Did you get any sleep?" Kit asked as Cyril held back a leafy branch, letting her pass ahead of him to the brook. The burbling water was just a dozen paces away now. It sparkled like a thousand tiny gems, creating a rippling pathway that raced over the moss-covered rocks.

"I did." It wasn't a lie exactly. He had gotten sleep, if only a few hours of it—the ones when it had been his turn to sleep with Kit pressed against him. But not sleeping was nothing new. Sleep brought too many memories. In some, he was caged like an animal, unable to spread his wings for years on end. In others, it was... worse. He'd been shocked the first time Kit's presence in his bed had quieted his mind. It was the only thing that ever did.

He'd never told her—or anyone— that. And it didn't seem like something to mention now either.

"Did you?" he asked. "I know the skirmishes made things difficult."

"I'd have gotten more if I hadn't spent an hour arguing with a bullheaded dragon," she muttered. Quinton hadn't let Kit put more of the Dragon Tears tonic onto his wounds, and she hadn't been happy. Cyril had left before that particular argument ended but apparently the discussion hadn't gone in Kit's favor. "He told me that if he wished to feel his flesh melting again, he'd toss himself into the flame and save us all the trouble," she confided.

"That sounds... descriptive."

"That sounds like a load of horseshit." She took off her boots to step in the water, but retreated after dipping her toes into the freezing water. Cyril stifled a laugh.

"In Quinton's defense, that tonic does burn like hell itself," he told her.

"Oh, that I believe a hundred percent," Kit said, squawking as she dunked her hair into the water and gave it a quick rinse. "I mean, just look at who gave it to us. What I don't buy is Quinton considering anything that makes him more miserable a bad thing. Can you turn around? I want to bathe and I'm not going inside there."

"I've seen you naked, nymph." In fact, he'd first touched her bare backside at a stream. Kit's embarrassed, surprised arousal had been adorable at the time. Back when she'd been skittish around the dragons while Cyril felt so stars-damned confident, taking his right to soothe her for granted.

Now, she glowered at him with no hint of fear. "It's not the same."

"I'm not turning my back on you while we are on the trial grounds. It's not safe."

She sighed, but settled for turning away and stripping down to the waist before using a small cloth to scrub herself clean. Water dripped from Kit's wet hair, running along the groves of her shoulder blades and making the tattoo there shimmer in morning light. As if the dragon inked on her skin was alive.

Despite her back being to him, Cyril was tall enough to see that Kit's breasts were reacting to the chill with predictable tightness—one that his balls uncomfortably echoed.

He quickly splashed some frigid water onto his face and steered the conversation away from the suddenly uncomfortable present moment. "Dragon Tears are difficult to come by, and Quinton's wounds will be mostly mended by now. I don't see the harm in saving what's left of the tonic in case a more dire need arises."

Kit stiffened. "You mean in case I get hurt."

"That's not what I said," Cyril hedged.

"It's what you meant."

It was. Only one of the five of them was mortal. "Is that so bad?" Cyril asked. "A mate saving medicine for the other half of his soul?"

Mate. Kit was Quinton's *mate* now. Not that Cyril was jealous. Mating to Quinton didn't make Kit like the rest of them any less. In fact, when it came to intimacy, Quinton had a great deal of ground to cover just to catch up to what Cyril and Kit had already done.

Cyril stifled a sigh as he scanned the treeline for any signs of trouble. Of course he was jealous. Not of Quinton and Kit per se, but from the vibrating connection that crackled between them now. Even when they were a breath away from taking each other's heads' off. Especially then.

He wasn't sure where he stood with Kit now. He wasn't her captor anymore obviously, and he wasn't her prince either. Was he her friend? Could he even claim such a title when she knew nothing about the dark side of him?

"Can you hand me my shirt please?" Kit asked. Cyril obeyed, bringing over the garment while Kit rang the remaining water from her blond-dyed hair. She shuddered as chilled water ran down her back, her full breasts jiggling. Cyril was about to step away while Kit refastened her chest binding, when the goose bumped skin along her spine caught his notice.

"Wait." He ran his hand over her back, following the

newly inked designs of Orion's tattoo. "The scars here. They are gone."

"What do you mean?" Kit asked.

"On the Phoenix, after I lashed you, there were some small scars left afterwards." Cyril's jaw tightened. The blood running down Kit's back that day had been a recent feature in his nightmares. "On a fae, the marks would have vanished completely, but human skin is more delicate. There were some marks left. Except now there aren't."

Kit shrugged, fastening her clothes. "Maybe they just took longer to heal. Unless you want to chalk it up to *Orion's will.*" She dropped her voice in imitation of the priest.

Despite his darker memories a moment earlier, Cyril chuckled.

"If it was her will, it was rather selective," Kit added, showing him her forearm where the irritated slave brand still remained.

"You really should stop scratching that," Cyril admonished.

Ignoring him, Kit pushed down her sleeve and tied her sash into place, sheathing the small dagger Quinton had given her. The blade hid nicely under the fabric's flaps and encapsulated everything that the nymph was: brave, honorable and very small.

"Glad as I am that you are armed," Cyril said, "please don't imagine that poking a dragon with that will accomplish much."

"You think I'm planning to attack a dragon with a dagger?"

"I think a great many things enter your mind," Cyril said honestly. "And a good number of them are not smart life choices."

"If you are going to start in on my returning to the trials, I'm going to test how well my little dagger works on your fae form," Kit snapped with enough irritation that Cyril thought she might be serious. A part of him even wanted to see her try. He'd never actually sparred with her. That was another thing only Quinton had done. But this wasn't the time.

He held up his hands. "I think we are past the point of arguing about your presence at the trials, don't you?"

"We are." Instead of being placated though, Kit took a step away. A flicker of hurt flashed over her face.

Cyril winced. "Kitterny... The humans mistreated you. Made you a slave." He cradled her forearm, uncovering the brand as if she needed the reminder. "And then we did the same to you, for all the choice you had. You only aligned with us to get your freedom. Once you had it, there seemed little reason for you to continue dancing to our tune. So we let you go."

Instead of being placated, Kit pulled away. "So your solution to my not having a choice before was to take another choice away from me?"

This was not going the way he'd intended. "We didn't think you'd *want* to stand up for either side after that.

Dragon or human. Even you must agree that's not unreasonable."

"You never came after me," she said quietly. "After all the talk of being pack, when Ettienne sent me out of your lives forever, you didn't even fight it."

"Fight to drag you into this rutting mess? Are you bloody insane?" Cyril's nostrils flared with frustration. "Whatever else you want to argue about, whatever else I'm guilty of—and believe me, I'm guilty of enough things to make you hate me ten times over—this I'm not apologizing for. Not for putting you before my life, or the pack, or the stars taken realm."

"Even if that's what I wanted?" Kit raised her chin defiantly. "Because, spoiler alert, it was. It's bad enough it never occurred to you that I might care about the actual future of the human race or the pack, it didn't even occur to you to ask."

"What about what we wanted then?" Cyril's voice rose along with his scales. He towered over Kit now, meeting her fierce glare with his own. "You think I want to see you put your life in danger? You think it isn't killing every single one of us to know that these blight forsaken trials care nothing for human lives? That we might lose you altogether?"

Kit's eyes flashed like a storm. "And if I want -"

"Start wanting something that won't kill you, and we'll talk about it!" Cyril's chest heaved, his words coming with harsh breaths. Behind him, the stream was rushing over the rocks, his magic unable to keep to itself. A violent wave of it picked up a loose stone, hurling it against the mountainside.

Someone cursed.

Cyril's pulse pounded in his head so loudly that it took him a whole heartbeat to realize the sound didn't come from Kit. Spinning about, Cyril shoved her behind him in one smooth motion, his hand going to the sword that he'd at least been smart enough to keep on him.

Blight take him. He'd gotten so worked up arguing, he'd not realized how much of a target the shouting was making of them. Well, he sure as hell realized it now.

Especially as two males rushed at them from the woods.

"Take cover," Cyril ordered, pointing across the small expanse of clearing toward the copse of trees on the other side.

For once, Kit did as she was told without argument.

Cyril barely had time to thank the stars for that small miracle before his blade met the first attacker's—a short stocky male with a mop of blond hair.

The sharp ring of steel on steel echoed in the stillness as Cyril's blade clashed with Blondie's, the force of the blow reverberating up his arm. Blondie tried to power through the parry, either because he thought he could win or just to buy his partner an advantage.

The second male, taller and leaner than his companion, aimed his weapon at Cyril's legs. He was fast, his savage grin lighting up a face with a crooked nose.

Cyril threw Blondie off just in time to leap over Nose's

blade. His heart quickened in his chest, the adrenaline spurring him forward. Landing softly, Cyril danced over the rugged terrain, maneuvering the attackers so they fell into line with each other, their separate assaults now a hindrance to their own advancement.

They tried to circle him again, their jabs and parries designed to wear Cyril down and test for weaknesses more than deliver a final blow. In another time Cyril would have been happy to oblige their game, but not now. Not with Kit here.

Cyril summoned his magic, the primal kind he'd not used in a great while—yesterday's demonstration in the meadow notwithstanding. The familiar rush of power coursed through his veins, wild and tempting. Easy to lose himself in. Too easy.

When Blondie rushed forward again, Cyril unleashed himself on the male. The magic hit Blondie square in the chest, sending him arching through the air to plop into the frigid stream. Water rushed to cover the male's face, forcing itself into his mouth.

With a guttural cry, Nose rushed forward, his blade arcing through the air.

Cyril spun, his sword and magic at the ready.

The mercurial clouds shifted then, the sun's rays suddenly reflecting off polished steel before a shadow fell over the field of battle once more.

But it wasn't from the clouds.

A surge of terror spilled into Cyril's blood as he realized

that it was a dragon in flight that had eclipsed the sun. The dragon that hunted not him, but Kit.

Blondie and Nose had been a distraction.

Cyril's cry echoed off the mountain as the great beast swooped down and snatched the still running Kit into its talons before carrying his catch off into the sky.

CHAPTER 14

Kit

*P*anic grips me as I'm yanked upwards, the ground receding at an alarming pace. My body dangles in the dragon's grip, its sharp talons digging into my flesh through the thin uniform. The wind screams past, cold and ruthless, whipping my hair around my face. The harsh buffet of the dragon's powerful wingbeats echoes in my ears, overwhelming the natural sounds of the world below. Everything but Cyril's call. Somehow I still hear that.

My captor banks a sharp right, and my stomach churns, my heartbeat erratic as the terrifying ascent evens out. Beneath me, the world is reduced to an abstract tapestry, the vibrantly green forest and the stone citadel blurring together into a whirl of colors. At this height, I don't dare thrash about lest the beast decides I'm more trouble than I'm worth to carry.

Through my terror riddled mind I register that the scales around the talons holding me are a rich brown color, not midnight black. It's not Geoffrey then. But it could still be someone from his pack or one allied with them. If that even matters. Dying is dying.

I draw a breath, surprised to find that it goes inside my lungs. I'd somehow forgotten that I can breathe. Then another thought occurs. I've actually been in this position before. Well, not this exact one, but probably closer than any other human has and lived to tell the tale. Now that I feel the unforgiving bite of the brown dragon's talons, I realize how careful Hauck had been when he'd carried me. Still, I'm alive. Which means this dragon doesn't want me dead. At least not yet.

Maybe he wants to share me with his packmates for breakfast.

Closing my eyes, I yank the bond Quinton and I share and then shout for Tavias with my mind. The communication has always been one way, but I've little to lose by trying. My mind races. Cyril saw me being taken, I remind myself. He'll come after me. He'd tell the others.

Unless he is hurt. He'd been fighting two dragons at once. Those weren't good odds. How long until—

We are coming. Tavias's mind voice sounds too calm for the raging wind. *Stay put.*

Relief rushes through me, followed closely by absurd indignation. Stay put? Where does he think I'm going to go?

A laugh I've no control over bubbles from my chest.

The dragon twists his massive neck, his slitted eyes giving me a confused glare.

"Tavias just told me to stay put," I tell the dragon. "Solid advice, don't you think?"

He snaps his jaw, barely missing taking my foot off at my ankle.

"You've got no sense of humor," I inform him. Actually, the dragon probably has as much of a sense of humor as I have a sense of reason.

I'm still contemplating this—which is better than dangling in frozen terror—when an ear piercing shriek fills the sky. I recognize the sound even before I see three forms shooting toward us, Quinton's silver dragon in the lead.

Three. Quinton. Hauck. Tavias. Where is Cyril?

Relief floods through me when I catch sight of blue scales flashing in the sun's rays, Cyril's dragon beating its great wings to catch up to the pack.

"We have company," I tell my ride.

The talons holding me dig tighter into my tender sides. I wince.

Quinton roars his fury, making the very air around us shudder. For how controlled Quinton keeps himself in his fae form, his dragon sways the other way, the primal rage emanating from him consuming everything. The pressure of it rushing through the mating bond makes it hard to breathe, much less think. We are really going to have to do something about that.

Quinton's dragon calls out again, the pack gaining on us. That part I like. The part I'm not so solid about is what in all the realms is supposed to happen when the four of them catch up. Attack the one being that's keeping me from falling to my death? And for that matter, what is Mister Brown Dragon intending to do with me? The moment I'm no longer in his possession, his life is bound to turn toward the shorter side. But what's the alternative? Ferry me around indefinitely? To what end?

Blinking against the wind, I try to take stock of where we are.

We are... still very high up. Below, the trial grounds roll by in a carpet of trees and mountains and valleys that would be beautiful if they weren't so far away. Ahead, the very air itself flashes with a strange rune. The marker noting the edge of the trial grounds, no doubt. The one that will kill me if I go past it.

Shit.

Wait. I force another breath into my lungs and remind myself that if Brown wanted me dead, he could have dropped me a hundred times over by now. He hasn't. So he is after something else. That, or I'm the equivalent of his new dog toy, with no plan beyond that.

The beating of the dragon's wings quickens, our trajectory never wavering from the barrier. My certainty that killing me is not the plan waivers. A lot. Whatever Brown's plan had been originally, it might have changed now to simple escape. Use me as a shield against getting shredded on this side of the barrier, then go past and keep going.

My heart quickens.

The flashing barrier comes closer with each wing beat.

I scream.

Brown banks. We swerve a blink before hitting the barrier. The world tilts beneath me, my breath hitching at the sharp change of direction—and then again as fresh horror of realization strikes me. This chase, it isn't about me at all. I'm nothing but a pawn, a piece of bait intended to lure my packmates out of bounds. And once they cross that glowing divide, they wouldn't be able to return.

My suspicions turn to terrifying certainty as I watch Quinton's sleek, silver form hurtle towards the boundary. His momentum, his speed, it's all too much. He is on a collision course with the divide, and there is nothing I can do but watch.

I can see the moment Quinton realizes his predicament. He screeches, desperately backflipping, his wings beating against the air with feral urgency. But it's no use. He's too close. Even I know it.

Just as my throat closes around a howl, a massive purple dragon streaks across the sky. Tavias. With a mighty roar, he crashes into Quinton, his body a battering ram designed to knock the silver dragon off his catastrophic course.

They collide with a thunderous crash and no grace, the impact echoing through the sky. Quinton careens off course, barely missing the boundary, while Tavias is spun away, his flight momentarily erratic before he regains control. Blood smears both the dragons' shining scales.

Emboldened by his near-success, Brown twists in the air, turning his attention to his next target. Cyril. My heart seizes as Brown begins his fatal dance once again, his large form banking and swerving, each move designed to lure Cyril toward disaster.

My fear over my predicament morphs to fury at Brown's plan. So he and his ilk think they can use me against my pack, do they? That I'm nothing but a lure on the end of a fishing pole? Ettienne might have predicted the others weaponizing me, but he forgot one thing. They all did: My males are my pack, and I am theirs. And there is strength in that. Claws in that.

I happen to be one of those claws.

"Hauck!" I shout over the wind.

Fortunately, the dragon's hearing is better than mine and the golden dragon turns toward me, his emerald eyes meeting mine with that familiar twinkle that takes me right back to the time that dragon and I spent in the clearing. The one when I had run my hands over his scales and marveled at his beauty without a shred of fear, because I trusted him. I hope Hauck's dragon remembers that day too, because I need him to return that trust now.

I call his name again and point beneath me.

Hauck dives down without hesitation.

That's my cue. Pulling out my toothpick of a dagger that

Cyril mocked, I do the one thing no one sane should—I jam the sharp blade into the sensitive webbing between the talons holding me.

The dragon screeches in pain, his claws opening on reflex.

And then I'm airborne.

My stomach drops as I free-fall through the air, the wind rushing loudly in my ears. Just as the ground begins to loom in terrifying clarity, a streak of gleaming gold appears beneath me. Hauck's dragon, banking out of the clouds like the mythical creature that he is. His massive body glides smoothly under my plummeting form, aligning with my fall.

It happens so fast, so seamlessly, that it's almost surreal. The jarring impact when I hit Hauck, the rush of relief flooding my senses, the lurch of my stomach as my abruptly arrested descent is replaced with the smooth, undulating movements of dragon flight.

Grabbing onto the scaled ridges of Hauck's shoulders, I throw one leg over to straddle him. His body is a solid mass beneath me, warm and very alive, the strong muscles flexing with each powerful wing beat.

Above us, echoes of battle roars reverberate through the morning air, followed by the fierce, almost rhythmic thuds of a violent skirmish. Tavias, Cyril and Quinton, doling out the consequences. If the vitriol I feel pulsating through the bond is any indication, the fight will end in blood. I crane my neck to look, but the motion unbalances me.

I feel it coming the moment before it happens. My grip

fails, my body sliding back, back, back along Hauck's spine, the scales of his back a slick slide beneath me. I struggle to grab hold of something, anything, but I'm no match for gravity and momentum. There's a moment of startling emptiness, the air rushing past me with a cool indifference, and then the world jerks back into focus as Hauck's talons close around me as if catching a sack of, well, turnips.

So much for making a respectable entrance back to the ground.

There is a small shaking sensation that gives me the distinct feeling that Hauck is... laughing.

I scowl at him.

Hauck snorts. Then his muscles contract and, before I can process it, I'm tossed back up, my body following the arc of his throw. The world spins in a wild swirl of color, a kaleidoscope of the sky, earth, and dragon. A gasp escapes me, half-surprise, half-exhilaration as Hauck comes up beneath me once more. This time, the jarring impact is familiar. I scramble for purchase, regaining my seat once more. My heart pounds in my chest like a wild drum before laughter ripples out of me, a wild and untamed sound that melds with the roars of the dragon battle above.

I'm flying. I'm bloody *flying*.

And stars, I like it.

Catching on to my mood, Hauck takes us into a looping spiral, repeating the human catch and release procedure when I inevitably lose my seat again. We are about to go for another round when two dragons, one blue and one amethyst rise up on either side of us, their fury palpable as they guide Hauck and me down to the ground.

I try to look contrite as I slide down Hauck's leg as if it were a shiny long slide, but despite my best intentions my grin gives me away. There are flashes of light all around me, Hauck, Tavias and Cyril returning to their fae forms. I don't ask where Quinton is. By the violence still echoing through our bond I suspect he is dismembering someone right now.

From the way Tavias is standing, he is of a mind to take similar action.

"I don't know which of the two of you I want to kill first." Tavias splits his growl between me and Hauck, who has his arm looped around my waist, the high from flight still clinging to us both like an intoxicating perfume.

"I mean if you are looking for recommendations, I'd suggest starting with that brown piece of shit that took me to begin with," I offer. Clearly, my sense of self-preservation is still on holiday, because even Tavias's palpable fury is unable to pierce through my daze of drunken rush coursing through my veins.

"I don't know," Hauck scratches the back of his head in mock concentration. "The last I saw of Quinton, that brown piece of shit was not a singular entity anymore. More like... "

"Diarrhea?" I suggest. A new bout of laughter escapes me, and I start wondering if maybe I did lose my mind some-where along the way. "Because, brown and—Oh stars." I meet Tavias's furious gaze and double over in manic laughter, tears stinging my eyes as I try and fail to control the bouts of mirth. "You know, because when Quinton went after the brown—"

"I think I have a clear image, thank you," Tavias says tersely. At the edge of my vision, I can see Cyril's tight mouth fight against a smile, as he does an admirable job of looking appropriately menacing. Tavias sighs and mutters something to the stars that sounds less than complimentary of both my and Hauck's intellect. "I imagine we should just be grateful that Hauck was there when that asshole decided to drop you from the sky."

"Oh, he didn't *decide* to drop me," I clarify. "I stabbed him." Cyril's eyes widen.

"You what?" Tavias clarifies.

I show him my dagger and make a stabbing motion. "You know, between the toes."

"You... You stabbed the dragon who was carrying you. Between the toes." Tavias annunciates each word. "So that he would let go. And you would fall. From the sky."

"Well, when you put it that way, it doesn't seem very smart at all," I mutter.

Tavias pinches the bridge of his nose and turns about military style before marching off, leaving me with Hauck and Cyril for company. Cyril and I still have words to exchange from our original conversation, but this isn't the time.

I clear my throat, looking up at Cyril. "Did you, err, want to scold us as well? While there is time before the first trial?"

"Yes, because that seems to be a strong deterrent factor for you both," Cyril intones evenly.

"Fair point. In our defense, this is a competitive advantage, isn't it?" I point out. "I mean, how many of the other humans will have ever ridden a dragon?"

"None," Cyril says dryly. "Which bodes well for their claim of intelligence to continue the dragon line."

"There is that," I point out again.

"You also didn't ride Hauck's dragon as much as fall off him. Repeatedly."

Practice makes perfect?

"Will you two at least promise to not do it again?" Cyril asks, though there is little hope in his voice.

"Would it make you feel better if we did?"

"Not if you lie," Cyril says.

"Well, then you need to make up your mind as to what you prefer," I say.

Before Cyril can come up with an answer though, three bells sound over the grounds, wringing all the humor from the air. The first trial was being called.

CHAPTER 15

Kit

*W*e meet Quinton at the base of the citadel. His gray uniform is soaked with blood that also speckles his face and hair. Before I can work out how much of it is his, a swarm of priests descends on us, wordlessly separating me and the other women from the dragon shifters. It's such an abrupt start to such a momentous event, that my mind is reeling while trying to process what's happening. The hooded figures leading us away offer no explanation. Fortunately, Cyril had flown back to the stream to get my boots, so at least I'm not going into the trial barefoot.

I quickly count the women as we walk, getting only to twenty two. A third of the competitors had died in the overnight skirmishes. Twelve dead since the pledge ball only a day ago. Or has it been a year?

I study the others' faces. Most are wearing expressions of frightened shock, though there are a few vacant stares and several resolutely determined ones. Bianca is one of the latter, walking like a queen to her rightful throne.

Using their staffs, the priests herd us along like a flock of sheep through a set of heavy double doors into the citadel. The scent of aged stone greets me and it takes my eyes a few seconds to adjust to the torch-lit gloom after the bright day outside. Another set of doors open on silent hinges and the sunlight is blazing into our eyes once more as we are led onto a platform at one end of a grand cheering arena.

If the start of the trial was silently abrupt, this moment makes up for it. The competition arena is colossal, its architecture wrapping around us and stretching toward the sky. Countless rows of stone seats fill the circumference, the spectators piled in and cheering. Beside the uniformed contestants, the sea of gowns and formal tunics are like splotches of color against canvas. I make out Ettienne in the front row, the king's face unreadable but intense. Autumn and Fionna are here too I realize, both clapping along with the others. The sound echoes off the stones, feeding on itself. Becoming even louder. More overwhelming. *Bom-Bom-Bo-bom. Bom-Bom-Bo-bom.*

And beneath all the din, there is a soft, barely noticeable sound that beckons me to leave the current festivities. Like a siren's lullaby. Or maybe that's just me hallucinating. After the morning I had, I'm allowed a little hallucination.

"Where are the dragons?" A girl next to me asks. She has ginger hair nearly the color of the orange trim on her uniform.

Someone points up, to where a translucent dome covers the top of the arena, its edges shimmering with an iridescent sheen that distorts the otherwise pristine blue sky. A dozen feet below the top of the dome, a metal catwalk stretches over the arena. That's where the males stand. Silhouetted by the sun, their faces are difficult to make out, but I can feel them. Or, more accurately, I can feel the bond with Quinton. It pulsates with anxiety. He is afraid for me. Not exactly comforting.

It makes me wonder what the males can see of the trial arena that I can't.

"Well, I've always been curious about what a mouse feels like with hawks circling above," the ginger girl says with a forced smile. Her pale face makes her freckles stand out. "Though if they are going to circle above us like that, they could at least offer cheese. Mice in a mousetrap should be offered cheese at the least."

"Cheese *and* wine," I agree.

A tiny giggle escapes her mouth before she clamps her hand over it, the women around us giving us dirty looks.

"I'm Leesandra," the girl offers her hand. "Or just Lee."

"Kit."

She snorts, her voice lowering to a whisper. "Oh, I know.

I mean anyone deaf, dumb and blind knows who you are. You've the dragon princes on your side. What are they like?"

"Dominating pains in my ass mostly," I whisper back. I feel like I've not had a normal conversation with a human my age since I've left the Agam estate. *The fact that this is my idea of a normal conversation is all kinds of messed up.*

Lee's face lights up in delight, drawing more dirty looks from the others.

I like her already. Clearing my throat, I return to surveying the trial grounds. From where we all are, on a platform at the east end of the oval, I can't see what the challenge is actually about, except that the center of the oval appears to be a large hole.

The sound of the gong ricochets off the stone walls, bringing with it an eerie silence. The spectators stop their cheering, turning their heads in unison to the imposing figure of the head priest. He stands atop a raised platform on the opposite side of the arena from us, his face shadowed beneath the cowl of his robe, the holy insignia of Orion gleaming on his chest.

"Subjects of the Goddess Orion," the priest's magic enhanced voice fills the arena, commanding and full of authority. "We gather here today to observe as our competitors prove their strength and wit in the first of the trials."

Subjects of the goddess? That feels bold to me, especially with the king of Massa'eve in attendance. But the priest doesn't ask my opinion as he continues in a poetic prose about Orion and fertility and being worthy. I want him to get to the point of the rules already.

It takes him a while, but eventually the priest swings his outstretched hand over the arena, guiding our attention from the east side platform where we stand to the west side one he orates from. "Your trial is simple yet formidable. The women must cross this arena to this platform on the west. Here, where the sun sets, shall the end—and new beginning —be found."

He pauses, letting the gravity of his words sink in. A few women exchange nervous glances, but Bianca's face remains composed, determined.

"But be warned," he adds, his voice dropping lower, the words heavy with foreboding. "The path will not be easy. Orion's favor is not given, it is earned. The pit before you is a testament to this. You must navigate its depths and rise victorious on the other side. Let the first trial begin."

With those final words, a wave of anticipation sweeps through the crowd. Lee and I exchange glances and walk two dozen feet to the edge of the platform, getting our first glimpse into the pit.

The challenge sprawling before us seems deceptively simple. It's a ridged path carved from the earth itself, a twisting serpent between one platform and the other. The walkway itself is two feet wide, but drops off sharply on either side, falling away into a pit that yawns open a good twenty feet below.

"Tell me I'm hallucinating and that isn't really a horse-sized worm." Lee points to a brown thing I'd thought was a pile of dirt.

But it isn't, not unless dirt slithers about and has rows of sharp teeth.

There are piranhas in the pit, Tavias's voice informs me. *Do not fall.*

"Piranhas," I tell her.

"Oh good. They have a name."

"And a stench." I pull my face away, the putrid stench rising up from the piranhas' layer prickling at the back of my throat. It smells like decay, like things long dead and forgotten.

"This is it? The great trial?" A girl with yellow trim around her uniform scoffs, pushing her way to the steps leading down to the start of the path. "You want to know if we can walk a two-foot ridge without breaking our necks? Fine." Without further ceremony, she steps onto the path with a confidence that I envy. She is probably one of the women who'd been training for this since childhood, her graceful unhurried steps making her seem to be out on an afternoon stroll.

The girl makes an uneventful turn around the first of the three bends in the path, and continues to the second with an increased bounce in her step.

"There is no way in hell it's that straight forward," Lee mutters.

I don't disagree, but several of the other women seem emboldened and take to the path. I tilt my head back to survey the tense bodies of the dragon shifters lining the catwalk. Apparent spectators. Except... Except the males standing there are already responsible for killing or running out a third of the packs. If none of them react to the crossing humans, we could all live. But the priests are counting on the competitors' own violence.

This is all kinds of messed up.

I'm proved right just as the women already on the path seem to find their cadence. There is a whip-crack of sound, and a dazzling streak of pure white energy leaps down, striking the earth. Lightning magic. The air splits with a terrifying crack, a blinding flash lights up the entire arena.

One of the women falls dead on impact but all lose their footing as the path convulses under the force of the impact. A cloud of dust and clumps of earth rise together with the screams. The path crumbles in two places, sending two more competitors off the side.

"What was that?" Lee asks.

I cover my face. The stench of ozone, sharp and metallic, fills the air, leaving a bitter tang on my tongue.

"That was the future king of Massa'eve," Bianca informs her, before turning to me. "Enjoy your stroll, Lady Kitterny."

Of course it was him who'd broken the fragile unspoken peace. Because the asshole couldn't bear the thought of anyone but his own pack getting through this.

Now that the possibility of safety for all is off the table, chaos breaks out in full. Flames roar to life from one shifter's command, snaking their way down towards the path. Before the fire can reach its target, a sudden surge of water rises from the pit's depth. The two elements meet in a clash. Hissing steam and reverberating magic spreads out like a shockwave. Rivers of wet earth roll down the path's sides, dragging two women toward the roused piranhas.

More attacks follow, some hitting the path, others meeting shields or elemental counter strikes.

"Stars." Lee's face pales. "My males... they don't have the power to go against someone like Geoffrey."

One of the women still on the path takes off at a sprint. I grip Lee's wrist as the runner makes it to the second bend before she is targeted in earnest. Geoffrey tries to send his lightning down again, but someone—presumably one of the males in her pack—throws up a shield to block the assault. My stomach clenches as the ground beneath the girl's feet gives way regardless.

She leaps over the hole. Pushes herself faster. Harder. Then she is on the west platform, safe and alive and panting. A shimmering shield that matches the one forming the dome repels any attack trying to smite her there.

Cheers and boos break out from the stands. The sound of clapping hands and stomping feet is nauseating. There is coin being exchanged. I bet there is. As if all this, all our lives, are nothing but a game.

You need to go next, Tavis says into my head. *Geoffrey is distracted. Go. Now.*

I grab Lee's hand. "We need to go now."

Fear pales Lee's face and she shoots a quick glance up to the catwalk.

Now, wildcat! Tavias mind shouts.

"I—"

"You are staying close to me and getting across," I tell her with all the authority I can muster. "We both are."

There is a static sensation along my skin as Lee and I pass through the invisible barrier that separates the arena from the safety of the platform. Immediately, I feel the coarse stone of the path under my boots. The path seems less steady than I expected. Narrow. The wind picks up around me, tugging at my clothes and hair, trying to upset my balance. Perhaps worse, the gust carries the stench from the pit below. The piranhas' rot is now mixed with the coppery tang of fresh blood.

Bile fills my throat. I want to wretch.

"We've got this." Lee squeezes my hand.

Holding on to Lee's hand, I inch forward along the path, testing each patch of ground before putting my full weight on it. My pack may protect us from above, but they can't keep the abused ground beneath our feet from giving way. More stench fills my lungs, dust from raging explosions gritting my nose and mouth and eyes. I bend, shielding my face with my free hand, my attention focused on one step after the other.

Fear courses through me, my body tense. Alert. Pelted with a storm of non-unending debris and screams of the injured. As horrible as those sounds are, the sudden silence at the end of those howls are worse still. I don't want to die. Not here. I shudder as a surge of magic hits the path a few paces in front of me, raising a fountain of rocks into the air. Something strikes my shin. My leg buckles. A sudden stab of pain drops me to the ground.

"Get up, Kit." Lee pulls desperately on my hand. "You have to get up."

I know she is right. I have to move no matter how much it hurts. I rise. Step. Falter.

"Kit!" I hear Lee's voice through a haze that I try to shake off. I can't. I think Tavias is shouting something into my mind as well, but I can't catch the words.

The bite mark on my breast tingles, calm confidence flowing like a lifeline into me. Quinton. I hear him. Not his words now, but the ones he'd said to me back at the inn. About me being the pack's best chance. About believing in me. That sensation and more flow into my soul, giving me the strength to push on. Keep moving. So I do.

Which is when Geoffrey turns his attention to me and lightning splits the air.

CHAPTER 16

Quinton

*E*ach pack was siloed. Quinton slammed into the invisible barrier blocking him from jumping down to the arena below, the force of the impact sending him backwards against a similar wall on the other side. His ribs were broken in at least two places, courtesy of his previous attempts to force his way through the partition. Now though, Quinton had a new reason to find an escape—Geoffrey needed killing.

On the serpentine parapet below, Kit struggled to get up. Cyril managed to redirect the worst of Geoffrey's murderous blow, but the assault had sent Kit into convulsions before showering her and her friend with a geyser of rocks and earth. She was injured. Her leg, her temple, her side. Kit's pain rolled through the bond.

Quinton soaked it up through the connection between them, feeding calm and confidence back toward his mate. Not an easy feat given that he was anything but calm. The confidence in her was the truth though. If anyone was able to survive, it was Kit. But she was only one mortal and she had Geoffrey and everyone else who was deciding to throw their lot in with the bastard obsidian dragon gunning for her.

She needed to get up. To move. That was the only way she could make it out alive.

"Lee. We have to go." Kit's voice sounded determined through a haze of pain. The arena was set up to allow the dragons to hear the humans below, but the reverse wasn't true. The humans could not hear the dragons, nor could the dragons speak to each other. Not with words at least. Actions though? Yes, those were clear.

Quinton bared his teeth at Geoffrey, then marked every other pack who leaned into Geoffrey's lead to harm Kit. A few had the sense to step back from the catwalk's edge, raising their palms into the air. Backing out of this fight. For now.

Geoffrey however only smiled like a self-satisfied snake preparing to swallow a mouse whole. The male's pupils were slitted and darkened to nearly all black, his pack standing smugly behind him.

Down below, Kit and Lee got to their feet, helping each

other along the path. Of their pack, Tavias and Cyril could both wield magic at a distance and in raw form, Hauck was piss poor without a direct connection with his element, and Quinton could do nothing without touch. Lee's pack was a well-meaning but weak bunch, barely equal to Hauck's power put together.

Quinton gathered all his power, threw it into the magical barrier, as if it were a living body he was testing for flaws. The magic vibrated at the intrusion. A start. If Quinton could get to and make an example of Geoffrey—

Hauck grabbed the front of Quinton's tunic and shoved him back. "You are no good to anyone dead," Hauck said, his voice more authoritative than Quinton had ever heard before. "And you are well on your way to getting there."

Quinton growled, but Hauck wasn't wrong. He focused on Kit. Being here, forced to watch her struggle, was a new kind of torture.

Flashes of destructive magic illuminated the arena below, searing the air in bolts of lightning and spears of air and catapulting stones. Cyril and Tavias threw themselves into shielding the humans from assaults, the crowd of spectators cheering whenever a new spear of magic found its way through their efforts.

Kit and her friend reached the final bend in the parapet, the air charged with so much raw power that Quinton felt it prickling his skin. Kit was close. Cyril and Tavias held fast. Seeing the final empty stretch of path sent Quinton's heart into a maddening rhythm.

"We've got this," Lee shouted. "We -"

Lee fell to the ground, a trickle of blood running down her temple. She rolled toward the edge. Kit grabbed Lee before she could topple over, nearly sending them both toward the piranhas' lair.

"Did that hurt?" Bianca called from behind them. Stars, it was her who'd thrown the stone. The first violence between the humans on the parapet.

"Are you insane?" Kit demanded, putting herself between Bianca and Lee. Quinton wasn't surprised. Kit was brave and kind to a fault. But she was also injured and that bravery might cost her her life.

"Insane? No. But I am smart." Bianca hurled a second stone, which Kit took on her shoulder. A pang of pain shot through the bond.

"Lee, go," Kit yelled, drawing her dagger. "Run."

Lee shook her head even as she swayed.

"Run," Kit ordered in a voice to rival a dragon. She was magnificent. "You are of no help to me. Go." She shoved Lee forward with more strength than Quinton thought she had. "Now."

Lee took off, moving with greater speed than Kit could have. Quinton would have blamed the girl for leaving, but Kit was right—Lee was too dazed to be of help. He wished Kit ran too, but her leg was much too hurt to outrun Bianca.

Raising her chin with a stubbornness Quinton knew all too well, Kit faced Bianca.

Bianca charged, aiming to strike Kit's injured side. Uninjured and larger, Bianca moved like someone trained for the kill.

Quinton poured all of himself into the bond.

Kit bladed herself on the narrow path, somehow dodging Bianca's headlong rush. "We don't all have to die for someone to win," Kit gasped out. "We aren't enemies."

"If you believe that, you are stupider than I thought." Bianca twisted, landing a punch on Kit's jaw.

Kit spun and swiped with her dagger. The blade whistled through the air, the crowd of spectators watching with stunned intensity. The magic assaults of the dragons halted too, Geoffrey not willing to accidentally send his own human stumbling off the parapet.

Kit's knife glistened, arching toward Bianca's heart. Quinton saw it. Kit did too. And damn it, she pulled the lethal blow.

Bianca jerked back just in time. A cruel smirk spread over her face. "Too slow, princess." Grabbing Kit's knife hand, Bianca used Kit's own momentum to pull her forward. Kit fell to her knees. Her knife fell from her hand.

Quinton gritted his teeth against Kit's pain, willing her to get up. To fight. To keep going.

Still on her knees, Kit lunged forward to tackle Bianca at her waist. The force pushed Bianca down to her back.

The crowd erupted with opinions, half booing and half cheering depending on whose side caught their fancy. Quinton went still, seeing what the crowd was yet to figure out. Kit didn't win that round at all.

He watched with impotent horror as Bianca, still on her back, jammed her feet into Kit's hips. She shoved up. Kit's lower body lifted into the air. Up. Up. And over the side of the parapet path.

Cheers roared from the stand, a contrast to the horrified silence of the pack. Bianca stood, panting and triumphant. She then turned away from the edge, resuming her run towards the end of the course, leaving Kit's fall in her wake.

Quinton shuddered, the arena swimming before him. Reaching out, he grasped the first arm he could. Hauck's. "She's alive," Quinton panted. "Hurt, but alive." He felt that much through the bond, along with the pulsating terror.

It was too dark to see Kit in the pit below, but the piranhas were now all gathering around the spot where Kit had fallen. They were dumb and mostly blind, but they could smell food.

Tavias loosed a jolt of flame. In the momentary light, they could make out Kit's body clinging to the nearly vertical face of the dropoff. Hauck had his hand out, shaking with effort but no vines responded to his plea.

Yet, a part of the dropoff beneath Kit shifted with excruciating slowness. A boulder started to jut out. What in the hell? None of the pack could do that. Quinton's attention shifted to find a pair of red headed brothers from Lee's pack panting with concentration as magic rippled around them. One male raised his face, sweat rolling down his temples, and nodded.

Just as the ledge grew large enough to be useful, a piranha

slithered onto it. Its maw of razor sharp teeth snapped eagerly.

The crowd gasped, the arena filled with the anticipation of carnage.

Quinton's throat closed. Kit was defenseless, her strength focused solely on holding onto the cliff face.

Just as the piranha made itself at home on the ledge forged for Kit, Quinton's mate did the unthinkable. She let go.

Quinton's world spun. He felt his heart drop with her, only Hauck's arms around him keeping him from lunging into the barrier again.

A shock of agony in his leg snapped Quinton back to the pit. The pain came from Kit's wound, not his own, as the girl bounced off the giant worm's springy body and launched herself up. She grabbed the edge of the parapet, her body still swinging from the force of her jump. With a grunt, she pulled herself up, lying flat on the narrow ledge. Alive and reaching for her fallen dagger.

CHAPTER 17

Kit

*E*verything is a blur of mud and motion, but I force
my eyes to focus on the platform that marks the
end of the course. I'm half conscious when I climb onto it,
every breath aching, but I'm here. I've made it. I'm aware of
the stillness around me, of the gazes of hundreds of eyes. The
calls and murmurs that are quieting down now, or maybe it
just feels that way now that the adrenaline is fading from my
senses. The hushed silence is palpable, broken only by the
distant cries of the women still on the parapet and the harsh
drumbeat of my heartbeat.

Then I hear it. A cheer, raw and thunderous, cutting
through the arena. My name. It's my name on the lips of

women and dragons and spectators alike. I can see Autumn clapping and shouting. Fionna too. And even Ettienne. The unexpected welcome pulls me from the precipice of unconsciousness. Somehow, my body conjures one more burst of strength and I get to my feet, using the wall for support.

Lee is there at once, her hand going around my waist to support me from the other side.

"What's happening?" I ask.

She grins, blood still streaking her bright red hair. "I think your little giant-worm trampoline trick has turned you into a crowd favorite," she says, shouting over the cheers. "Or it could be that you put yourself in danger to save my life, but knowing this crowd it's probably the former."

I snort. Because she is probably right.

On the other side of the platform, Bianca glares daggers at me.

"Can't please everyone," I murmur to Lee and give Bianca a saccharine smile. It feels... good. To stand here, having faced down a storm and survived. It feels like being a warrior instead of a victim.

As soon as the other women finish—one way or the other—the priests declare the trial over and the dragons are released from whatever restraints must have held them in place. Tavias, Hauck, Cyril and Quinton surround me so quickly that my head spins.

"You did well, wildcat." Tavias tries to pick me up but I shake my head at him, wanting to stand on my own two feet.

Well, one foot. My leg still hurts too much to put pressure on it. The males oblige by surrounding me with support, Quinton channeling what magic he can into healing me. The fact that his ministrations do nothing is worrisome, but I know this isn't the time to question the dragon.

The head priest launches into another of his speeches, something about us having pleased the Goddess Orion and how proud and grateful we should be about that.

I exchange a look with Lee. Women are dead and injured, yet we should be grateful that this little game pleased the priests' deity? I clamp my jaw shut lest my disgust with the priests leads me to make a poor life choice and try not to listen to his speech.

Ignoring him is easier than I expected. I'm hurt and I'm tired and there is soft music playing.

"I know that song," I murmur.

"We need to get her out of here." Quinton's hand is against my side again, his magic seeping into me.

I pull Quinton's hand away. He's barely able to stand himself.

He tries to put his hand right back but fortunately the priests release us just then and we move on to a new disagreement.

"I don't want to be carried," I tell Tavias, who is gearing up to do just that. Having just felt like a warrior, I don't want to go back to being lugged around like a turnip sack.

"Have you learned to fly while I wasn't watching?" Tavias

inquires with overstated patience. "Because your leg can't hold you."

"Just give me an hour to rest and I'll deal with the leg," Quinton insists.

"I can fly her," Hauck offers to the immediate uniform rejection from Tavias, Cyril and Quinton. I'm with Hauck though, and the rest of the pack finally relents to allowing him to ferry me up in his talons—no one trusting either me or him to let me ride mounted.

That turns out to be a wise decision, because somewhere between take off and landing I lose consciousness. When I'm aware of my surroundings again, I'm back at camp, laying on a sleeping pallet. Naked.

Hauck grins. "There she is."

"What are you doing?" I demand, sitting up and grabbing a blanket to cover myself. Seeing a bowl of water and washcloth beside him—and the fact that I'm no longer covered with grime —gives me my answer before he needs to explain. My cheeks heat, even though the males have seen me naked plenty of times.

I raise my chin, going for a measure of dignity. "So what's the damage?"

"Well, your piranha trick nearly made my balls explode," Hauck says. "There is still a threat of that by the way. So if you'd like to—*ooff*." He cuts off as Cyril smacks him.

"Better than expected," Tavias tells me. "The leg isn't broken. There is a deep gash along your ribs that we'll suture, but nothing vital was struck. You were lucky."

I don't feel lucky. Especially with Tavias's plan of running a sharp needle through my flesh over and over. I'm not sure the males, who've had much worse done to them over the years, would appreciate that though.

"I want her out," Quinton says from the back corner of the shelter, where he's been lurking. He looks awful. Worse than the bloody mess that he was before the trials even started. Hell, he might be worse off than I am just now.

Tavias turns toward him. "Of the shelter?"

"Out of the trials."

"After all the trouble I just went through to stay in?" I sigh when he doesn't even smile. "I don't believe that particular option exists."

"It does." Quinton's certainty makes a shiver run over my skin. "If there are no other competitors, there are no more trials."

I pinch the bridge of my nose. "Right, well, I vote against mass murder." Even if Quinton's plan wasn't suicidal, which it was, it would make us no better than Geoffrey. Lee and her pack and the others like them didn't deserve to die. Hell, none of us here deserve to die. A fact which seems to be lost on the priests of Orion. "Speaking of homicidal sociopaths, how do the priests of Orion have all this magic that no one else does?"

Everyone turns to Cyril.

"Am I the only one who paid attention at any lessons?" he asks.

"I paid attention," Tavias says a little too pointedly. "At the ones that concerned me."

Cyril ignores him and turns to me. "Long ago, when the dragons' fertility was just starting to wane, Prince Emric fell for the stunning Illiana. Star-crossed love, all that. All is good until their pup doesn't make it. Twice. Illiana's heartbreak is so profound, Emric fears she'll fade away.

"Emric, in his desperation, pleads with Orion to help Illiana and the other dragons facing the same plight. The goddess is touched. She guides Emric to a sacred ground with flowers that, when brewed into an elixir, can restore fertility. He brews the elixir, Illiana drinks it. They have a pup. But of course, making a deal with a god always has a price."

I frown. "Let me guess. Drinking the elixir made Illiana mortal?"

Cyril gives me an approving nod. "Exactly. Illiana becomes mortal and Emric is shackled to the sacred grounds for eternity, becoming the first priest of Orion, empowered by her blood but chained to her temple."

"It's a good legend, but where is the truth?" I ask. "The elixir doesn't make dragons mortal."

"No, but it only works on mortals. As with any legend, there is some truth and some embellishment. What we do know is that the priests are linked to the citadel, and they're the only ones who can tap into its magic. In return, they're tethered to the place like a dog to a post. They never leave these grounds except for the pledge ceremony. On the practical side, this arrangement ensures the priests can't angle for the throne and the elixir isn't a constant battleground. So, the trials, as vicious as they are, are the lesser of two evils."

"That's... well, that's sad all around." I shift my blanket and wince, drawing Quinton's attention like an arrow. "How long do we have until the next trial, you think?" I ask before he can make some comment I don't want.

Quinton's gaze hardens. "Could you not hear the priest?"

"I chose not to listen to the priest," I tell him.

"There will be a celebration of the first trial victors in a week," Cyril says, cutting off whatever Quinton is about to say. "The second trial will be a week following that. You've some time to heal."

"Speaking of healing." Tavias draws the medical satchel toward himself. The sharp glint of the needle sends my stomach roiling. He pushes on my shoulder gently. "Lie down and we'll get this over with."

The bile in my stomach threatens to crawl up my throat. I don't think—I know—I'm not going to take this part with any grace and really don't want an audience for the spectacle. "Why don't you all go hunt a rabbit or something?" I tell the other males.

Hauck's brows knit together, and I can see the protest forming on his lips. Before he can voice it though, Tavias takes one glance at me and actually backs me up.

"Out," he orders the other males. "Now. Even you." The last is pointed toward Quinton who is dark with fury.

They leave reluctantly, Cyril and Hauck dragging

Quinton with them and I let out a sigh of short lived relief. I will embarrass myself, but at least it will be in relative private.

"You are wrong, you know," Tavias says quietly once the others are gone. "To have made them leave."

I blink. "Then why did you help?"

He snorts, and moves closer to me. His hands are competent as he lowers me onto the palate, positioning my body to give him the best access to the wound. "Because I'm a general who spent most of my life on a field of battle. You think you are the first young warrior I've met whose fear of a needle is matched only by their terror of looking weak?"

I let out a shaky breath. "Am I that transparent?"

"No, I'm just that experienced." Tavias strokes my hair gently. "But they are your pack. Their thoughts—their only thoughts—are of giving you comfort. I'll do my best with giving you the same, but next time you might find it easier to be cradled in their arms. And you deserve no less."

I swallow. It's not as easy as he makes it seem. "When I crawled onto that platform, when I stood up and the crowd cheered, it felt good," I whisper. "I liked it. Feeling strong. Having all those people *see* me as strong."

"All those people only saw the truth that our pack already knows, wildcat," Tavias says without hesitation. "Hell, I think you showed the priests up, beating them at their game of making all of us into nothing but playthings."

Tavias's thumb brushes my cheek and his voice drops to a

whisper. "I know appearances are important. Vitally so… It's… It's one of the reasons I want to be Massa'eve's general, not its king. That's not something anyone outside our pack knows. But now you do. I trust you, wildcat. You can trust us too."

CHAPTER 18

Kit

*T*he celestial hall is an echo of the grand ballroom at the Massa'eve palace, with one notable exception. If the latter is built to celebrate the monarchy and the throne, the former elevates priests without even the pretense of subtlety. Magic infused glowing orbs hover beneath the vaulted ceilings and raised statues of hooded followers of Orion look down at the proceedings below. Long tables laden with spiced meats, aged cheeses and fresh fruit stretch along the perimeter, their midnight blue tablecloths flowing down to the marble floor.

We've all been provided with gowns and formal wear for the gathering and my purple chiffon dress flows airily around my thighs, covering what remains of my bruises.

My stomach growls loudly enough to make Hauck grin. With the males' hunting we've not gone hungry, but this is a feast. A feast with guests. My attention swims through the sea of people who I presume to be Massa'eve officials and friends and family of the surviving competitors. Ettienne is here, his chillingly handsome form towering over most others. So is Salazar.

"We are down to twelve packs," Cyril remarks. I wince. Some of those who'd finished the first trial must have succumbed to their injuries after all.

Or else been hunted down by the stronger packs. I search for ginger hair in the crowd and am relieved to find Lee and her males off in the corner.

"Prince Tavias. Lady Kitterny."

I jump, not having seen Autumn gliding over. She gives Tavias a respectful curtsy and inclines her head to the rest of us. Quinton ignores the courtesy until Cyril knocks him on the shoulder. Only then does he condescend to give Autumn the briefest of irritated acknowledgements.

She manages to look down her nose at him despite her tiny height.

"My apologies for my brother," Tavias says. "It has been a trying few weeks."

"Indeed," Autumn replies smoothly. Standing behind her, Fionna presses her lips together.

"My congratulations to you for successfully passing the first trial," Autumn continues. "Not that I expected any other outcome. Would you do me the honor of introducing your lady?"

"Of course." Tavias executes a courtly bow. "Lady Autumn, may I present Lady Kitterny, my pack's bride apparent. Lady Kitterny, allow me to introduce her highness, the Lady Autumn of the Slate Court. She is here on a diplomatic voyage, and I understand has a scholarly interest in tracing the dragons origins."

"Leave it to a dragon to make that sound so boring," Autumn says. "But His Highness isn't wrong. I am especially intrigued by the trials. In fact, I was hoping you might indulge me with your account of the first one? What it was like from the competitor's perspective?"

I see both Tavias and Cyril tense protectively.

"I don't imagine the lady wishes to relive that particular experience just now," Tavias says, his body already starting to blade between Autumn and me.

"I don't mind at all," I say quickly as I step around him. "But only if the princess might tell me about Queen Leralynn in turn. She is a legend."

That appeases the males long enough for Autumn to draw me away from them before more objections can sprout. They still watch me closely though. All except Quinton, who looks bored. Him and Hauck, who is splitting his attention between me and the wine being brought in.

There is little privacy to be found in the celestial hall, but Autumn leads me toward the food. We bypass the main course and stop directly at the dessert table, where she snatches up a plate of chocolate cake for the both of us.

"Don't drink the wine," she warns. "It's moonberry. Makes humans lose their wits along with their inhibitions."

"I'll keep that in mind." It's hard not to throw my arms around her, especially as she takes a mouthful of chocolate cake and moans in pleasure. I only spent a day with Autumn, but she already feels like a trusted friend. My attention snags on Fionna, standing a few paces away. Running interference for us. So she found a place for herself after all—one at Autumn's side.

I expect Autumn to ask something about the trials, but that's not the question that comes out, her voice low and quick. "The brand on your wrist. How did you get it exactly? No, don't touch it. Don't even look at your forearm. Just answer."

Not the question I was expecting. My brows crease. "It's been on me as long as I can remember, really."

Autumn purses her lips. "Surely you would recall getting something as painful as a brand."

I blink. Yes, of course. "I remember it hurting a great deal," I say, the memory of the pain flashing through me just then. "I was... My mother gave me up to an elderly couple. And then they sold me to the Agam estate. And I was branded somewhere during that time."

"But you don't recall the actual instance?"

"Of course I do. No one could forget that." My thoughts

keep circling on me. Of course I remember. How could I not. Wait. "I think my mother paid extra for a sleeping potion."

"But wasn't it the elderly couple who sold you?" Autumn counters as the musicians at the other end of the hall start playing and the center of the room fills with dancing couples. "And if you were asleep, how do you remember it hurting?"

Good points. All of them. I think back to the branding and my thoughts circle again. "I think I blocked out the details. Why do you ask?"

A richly dressed male holds his hand out to Fionna, drawing her to the dance floor.

"Are all the slave brands the same?" Autumn asks. "Exactly the same?"

"The two overlapping circles are the universal symbol, yes. I guess there would be slight variations based on the smith who makes the brand. And then the scar tissue changes it a bit. Again, why?"

Autumn speaks even quicker than she usually does. "Two circles, when overlapped in a particular way, form a binding rune." She gestures with her fork. "In simple terms, there are two schools of magic. Nearly everyone uses elemental power —magic that's inside them, usually tied to an element. Quinn's blood magic, and Cyril's rawer magic, the tiny puffs of air magic the women here are expected to have. The second school uses runes to channel magic from one source to another—that is how wards and the occasional magical amulets are set up." She winces. "Don't get me started on amulets and how those go wrong. Anyway, rune magic is extremely complex and precise. Tattoos from the pledge ball —rune magic."

"So the priests use rune magic," I say, thinking of Cyril's tale. "Given that they are tied to one place for their whole lives, I imagine it leaves them with plenty of time to study arcane arts. Still not seeing what that has to do with me though. All slaves are branded the same where I live. If the design originates from a rune, so what?"

Autumn's attention focuses on something behind me and she drops into a deep curtsy. "Your majesty."

Shit.

"Princess Autumn." Ettienne inclines his head with smooth politeness. "I hope you are enjoying the... cake?"

I realize that sometime during our conversation Autumn had snagged two more pieces and is unabashedly enjoying every bite. "Indeed," she confirms. "I find eating chocolate more relaxing than watching innocent women be slaughtered at any rate." She holds up her plate. "Happy to share."

Ettienne seems to fight a smile, but demurs, turning to me instead. "May I have this dance?"

I think I'd rather repeat the first trial than dance with Ettienne, but that seems like an undiplomatic thing to point out. I take his hand, reminding myself that he can't make good on his death promise here and now—which should make me feel better, and doesn't really. Ettienne's hand on my waist seems to burn through my gown's fabric. "I'm afraid my dancing may not be up to your standards, your majesty," I murmur.

"All you need to do is follow." Ettienne replies. "Though I understand that's a challenge for you." He steps into the music. To my annoyance, Ettienne is a smooth dancer with a lead even I can follow. "How are you holding up?"

"Alive. Sorry to disappoint."

Ettienne steps closer, his lips nearly at my ear. "I'm not your enemy Kitterny. Hard as you may find it to believe."

"My mistake. I must have misinterpreted things when you sent Quinton to kill me."

"A miscalculation on my part." Ettienne shrugs a shoulder. "I made a decision based on what I knew at the time."

"Does that mean you regret ordering me killed or sending Quinton to do it?"

"Do all my sons find your fiery insolence attractive?"

"I believe Cyril would prefer I chose my words with greater care. Tavias might as well. I've never asked."

Ettienne looks like he is holding back a laugh, the tips of his scales flashing a shade of silver. "Indeed. But we all must play the cards we were dealt now."

"I take it I'm one of those cards for you. How do you intend to play me?"

"I've not yet decided," Ettienne says with an honesty I didn't expect. "But at the moment your staying alive appears to suit both our interests."

"I'm pleased we agree on that at least." For however long it lasts.

Ettienne lifts his arm, guiding me to turn under it. When he reclaims me again, his gaze watches my face intently. It's disconcerting. This whole game is.

"What do you want from me, your majesty?" I just ask it.

Ettienne nods. "Keep my sons alive, please."

I give a small snort. "I believe it is them who are keeping me alive in this particular set up."

Ettienne's voice drops, stripping all humor. "That is where you're wrong, little human. Anyone with eyes can see as much. It is you who is truly keeping them alive. You are their greatest weakness, and their greatest strength. All rolled into one. There is a responsibility that comes with power such as that."

"May I cut in?" Despite phrasing it as a question, Quinton shoulders his father out of the way and takes me into his protective arms. Quinton's eyes keep moving around the ballroom the entire dance, as if scanning for threats lurking behind beverage tables and marble columns. Despite his grace, it's like dancing with a bodyguard. The moment the song finished, Tavias steps in to fill Quinton's place, then Cyril. They are all the same. Tense. As if they know something I don't.

CHAPTER 19

Kit

I am really starting to hate the sound of the gong, more so because it is deceptively beautiful with full rich notes that vibrate through the whole room.

Music stops. The couples currently out on the floor retreat to the sides of the open space, Tavias nudging me along as well. The head priest steps out and draws his amplification signal in the air before launching into another speech on the greatness of Orion and tradition and the trials. It's when I see some suppressed smiles from packs and visitors that my body tenses with foreboding. A moment later, I'm proven right.

"Fertility is our goal and hope and guiding light," the priest intones, raising his staff. The hood covers his head, but the tattooed skin of his face is still visible. Servants come in, shifting tables around to clear many of them. "Now has come the time for our packs to show, before Orion and the dragon kind, that the human brides they selected are indeed capable of fulfilling such a destiny."

"What does he mean exactly?" I ask, my stomach tight as I turn to Tavias.

"I think you know," Tavias answers gently.

I swallow. I do know. It was one of the things that the dragons had made clear from the beginning of this—while no one knows what the trials involve specifically, there is always a constant: the dragon packs and their brides will be expected to couple before the priests to demonstrate their compatibility despite the usual difficulties of the anatomies. Hell, the pack had spent weeks on the Phoenix preparing my body for this moment. And it was one of the things Cordelia had confessed about her training before she died.

"You knew this was going to happen at the feast," I accuse.

Tavias nods. "I strongly suspected."

"And you didn't think to tell me?"

"If you'd thought about it, you'd have strongly suspected as well," he says, not without understanding. "If you chose not to, we didn't see a reason to make you fret more than you did already."

He moves closer to me, his hands stroking my arms. "It will be alright, wildcat. Just focus on us. You are ready. And we've a few ways of making extra sure we have you—"

"Please, no. Not this. Not here." A desperation filled plea

trickles over the room. Tavias and I both turn to see a woman in a green dress. Tears roll down her face as two males hold her on either side, while a third strokes himself into hardness. "I don't want to do this." She twists as much as she is able toward the priests, begging them for reprieve.

"Get your human under control, Ulio," the priest orders the green pack leader—the one who still has his cock hanging out.

"Please," the woman turns to the priest and throws her forehead to the floor. "I don't want them to rut me here. Please. You can make them stop. I know you can. I'll do it in private. Just don't make me do it here."

The green pack leader backhands the woman into silence.

I'm moving before I know that I'm doing so. There is a ferocious roaring in my ears and a dagger in my hand, the one with the engraving of a rose. One step and I'm away from Tavias. Two and I've got my arm cocked. Three as my dagger and my words fly.

"Do not touch her," I shout to the suddenly silent room. The knife flies right at the dragon's chest.

He twists, catching the blade before it can so much as nick his skin then turns with a slowness that carries menace in every line of his body. I can feel Tavias and the others rushing forward toward me and know I've little time left. "She is supposed to be a bride not a slave," I yell. "She said no."

Quinton's arms close around me. "Quiet, human," he says into my ear. But we all know that it's like closing the barn door after the horse has already run. The woman is on the floor, crying softly. The crowd is brimming with fury. The priest... the priest moves with a kind of slowness that makes me wonder if he isn't enjoying the power.

"Pack leader Ulio," the head priest says, turning to the green dragon leader. "If you cannot control the human, disqualify her."

Disqualify. That means death. That's what the tattoos of Orion do. Shit, what did I think was going to happen?

Ulio bows, stuffs himself back into his trousers and brings a goblet of wine from the table. He crouches beside the cowering woman and thrusts the wine into her hands. "Drink," he orders, his tone gentling. "You are alright, Skyler. Slow breaths and deep sips. This will help."

The screaming girl nods and takes the goblet with both hands, taking a deep drink. Her breath slows just a few heartbeats later, her eyes taking on a glazed look. By the time Ulio pulls the goblet from her hands, Skyler is pulling on the bodice of her dress complaining about the heat. No wonder Autumn told me to stay away. Ulio makes his apologies to the priests, assuring them that there will be no more problems from his side.

That's when the entirety of the ballroom turns to me. Quinton's breath is tights on the back of my neck and there is dread crawling through the bond between us. His arms around me are iron bands, but I know they will not be able to protect me.

"Pack leader Tavias," the head priest says, turning our

way. "Your human has attacked another within the citadel and has violated our sacred rite. It is only because her clumsy attempt was so doomed from the start that the Goddess Orion has not exacted vengeance and her mark hasn't taken her life."

Shit. I'd totally forgotten about that part of the rule.

"However, it is unclear to us that the human you brought understands and submits to these trials."

"I accept full responsibility for the woman," Tavias steps forward, blocking me with his body. "It was my duty to keep her in line and I failed. I am ready for whatever punishment you and the goddess believe is just."

"You were not the one to assault Ulio's pack," the Priest points out. "You were not the one to insult us and the goddess."

"We do not punish a horse for a rider's error," Tavias says. "Clearly, the failure lies with me. It was my duty to control what bride I selected and trained. The failure is mine and mine alone. Please do me the honor of allowing me to pay for the insult in whatever way you see fit."

No.

The priest rocks back on his heels considering the situation, his attention narrowing on where Quinton's arms surround me. I try to read the priest's face, but the shadows and tattoos make it near impossible. The priest turns, counseling with two others of the order for several minutes while the ballroom waits. Then he turns back and orders a space in the very center of the ballroom to be cleared.

"Pack leader Tavias," the priest says. "Seeing as Orion chose not to end the girl's life at once, we too shall grant you a chance at redeeming your standing. Show us all that you hold the leash on this human you brought. Re-establish your full control before us, and leave us with no doubt of her submission. Then, and only then, shall we not disqualify her from the rite."

CHAPTER 20

Kit

The hall watches intently as Tavias turns on his heels and strides toward me with measured steps.

I straighten my spine and nod at him. I fucked up. I know I did. I knew where we were and why and the expectations—and instead of taking one moment to think about it all, I acted without thinking. I wanted to protect someone, and instead I endangered so many more.

Whatever Tavais needs to do to me now to get us out of this mess I'll understand. I want him to know that.

"Hurt her and I'll kill you." Quinton's warning is so quiet that only Tavias and I can hear him. No, not a warning, a promise.

Tavias gives him an emotionless look, then focuses on me. He places his large calloused hand on my cheek, his purple eyes penetrating into me. "I'm not going to hurt you, wildcat," Tavias says, the words just loud enough to be heard by me and the pack. "But I will destroy you until you are a submissive ragdoll writhing with mindless need. I'm sorry."

I've no idea how one is supposed to react to that declaration, but my body tenses and heats at once. Not that it actually matters. There is not much choice.

There is a low rumbling growl that comes from Quinton as Tavias grasps my elbow and pulls me from his arms.

"Restrain him if you must," Tavias orders Cyril and Hauck, with no more trace of emotion that he had earlier. "No one interferes with us. When your cocks are required, I'll let you know."

I try not to let the shiver of anxiety that rushed through take hold, but I can't help it.

"You are to keep your mouth shut," Tavias instructs me aloud. There is dominance in his voice and his shoulders widen in that way he has when he wants to make himself even bigger than he already is. "And keep your attention on me."

Tavias brings me to the center of the room, before the hundreds of eyes that are to watch as I am taught to submit to the dragon's power. I wish he'd just get it over with and tell me what he intends to do. I try to tell him that I don't hold him to the promise he'd made earlier. If a beating is coming, and it must be, then I understand. But he's told me not to speak so I keep my words to myself.

"I require a table," Tavias tells the servants.

One is immediately procured and placed in front of him.

"I also require wine."

"No," says the priest. "That is not the submission we seek."

Tavias bows to the priest. "I did not doubt that. I assure you, the wine is not for drinking."

Come again?

Tavias doesn't elaborate though, not even inside my mind. I don't understand his silence, which makes my nerves fire more with every passing heartbeat. Tavias turns to me.

"Strip," he orders, his mind adding in a tone no less hard. *Look at me as you do.*

I try to tune out the fact that there are hundreds of people watching as I pull off my dress. The fabric pools on the floor in a puddle of amethyst chiffon that I thought was so pretty. My shift comes next. My chest binding. My underthings. Each piece of clothing comes off like a bit of armor being stripped away. The crowd is starting to move about now, settling in for the show. A clink of glass as wine is poured. A chuckle as someone contemplates my ass. My skin heats.

Keep your attention on me, Tavias snaps inside my mind. *Or there will be a pink handprint on that full backside.*

I draw in a sharp little breath. Tavias has a wicked way of using that hand of his, that makes me want to rip his cock off and ride it all at the same time. He's bent me over before, doling out stings of pain that morphed into pleasure that had me dripping for no logical reason at all. He's done more with me. But right now... I feel only my heart pounding against my ribs.

I drape my hands over my front, covering myself the best I can.

"Hands at your sides." Stepping closer to me, Tavias kicks my legs apart, opening me farther. I gasp. His hand moves possessively over my skin, around the swells of my breasts and down my midline. *Beautiful,* he says into my mind. *And all mine.*

His hand slips lower, cupping my mound. I want to cover myself, but I don't dare move. He slips his hand between my legs and folds, then slips a finger into my channel. I'm anxious and dry, and the intrusion makes me want to cringe but I don't. Tavias's lips tighten into a line.

He picks up a sash from my discarded dress and ties it over my eyes, blocking out the sight of the room around us. The disorientation is immediate, my attention shifting immediately to my other senses. Tavias's scent consumes me, his hands on my hips lifting me onto a hard surface. The table he'd ordered brought for a reason I still don't know why. He lays me down on my back, spreading my arms and legs out and away from me.

"We are going to show everyone just how submissive you can be, wildcat," he says. "So you are not going to move a muscle from here. And you will take everything that I give you."

There is a velvety texture to Tavias's threat that makes a

new kind of shiver run over my skin. Without anything else to concentrate on, I strain to hear the sounds around me. Tavias' footsteps retreat then return a moment later. I smell wax. A candle. And its heat is *very* close to my skin.

CHAPTER 21

Tavias

*H*olding the candle close to Kit's skin, Tavias moved all around her body. Kit's naked form shuddered softly, her pale skin stretched taut across delicious hip bones and soft curves. Her breasts were full and round, nipples pebbled in the cool air. Tavias's mouth watered at the thought of tasting them, teasing the sensitive buds with tongue and teeth until she writhed beneath him. But that would have to wait. For now he needed to capture her attention in a way that the dryness between her legs said he hadn't done yet. He'd hoped the blindfold and heat would do the trick, but it wasn't enough. He felt it.

This was a lot for Kit. The hundreds of people looking on, the looming consequences, the too many thoughts churning in that brilliant and brave mind of hers. That last would be the hardest hurdle to conquer for them both. Especially given Kit's recent confessions. She thought her strength was somehow linked to appearance and going at it alone. Probably Quinton's rutting influence.

Unfortunately, she picked an inconvenient time to pick up his bad habits.

Too late now.

He reached out and spread her farther, opening her legs as far as the table would allow. She swallowed and he traced the curve of her hip.

He pulled her blindfold off, opting for the connection of their gazes. "Eyes on me," Tavias ordered, sliding his hand up to cup one full breast, testing its weight in his palm. He brushed his thumb over her nipple. Kit jumped at the contact. Tavias clicked his tongue in disapproval. "I said, do not move."

Releasing Kit's breast, he repositioned her wrists over her head, regarding her again as he decided his next move. This time Kit's gaze tracked him as he walked around and picked up the pitcher of moonberry wine, the spicy sweet aroma filling his nostrils. Tilting the pitcher over Kit's prone form, he poured the crimson liquid in careful patterns that encircled her breasts and trickled between her spread thighs.

Kit gasped softly, her stomach tensing as the liquid pooled in her belly button. It was lovely, really. Hauck's britches were likely straining with desire to lap it from there just then. But that wasn't going to happen.

"Be very very still," Tavias reminded, putting an edge of bite behind the order. With a thought, he conjured a flame and held it to Kit's breast.

The wine ignited, flames dancing across her skin. Kit cried out, but Tavias knew that it was fear and shock, not pain, that rang in her voice. The fire licked at her but did not burn, Tavias's magic keeping it controlled.

Kit whimpered, staying so very still that her whole body nearly trembled from the effort. Yes, Tavias had her full undivided attention now. Good. That's what he needed. He moved the flame down her body, setting small fires that burned hot and bright before dying out, only to be rekindled elsewhere.

Kit's racing heart eased as reality sank into her, her scent of fear replaced by wonder laced with healthy anxiety. The flames illuminated her body, casting dancing shadows across her skin. Tavias watched the flame carefully, tempering the interplay of fire and flesh.

Small sounds of the rest of the hall separated into the background, the tiny gasps of other humans and growls from the dragons, the clinks of servants cleaning up and musicians storing away their instruments. Tavias heard it all and pushed it away. As much attention as he demanded from Kit, he needed to give as much to her. Especially since they were only getting started.

He picked up the pitcher again, this time trailing the liquid between Kit's open thighs and so very close to the thatch of golden curls nestled there. Soon—sooner than Kit thought—sweet nectar would weigh them down. Tavias could already scent hints of her arousal, the musky perfume intoxicating as it reached his heightened senses. For now though, Kit's eyes were widening in shock.

A soft whimper escaped her parted lips, her desperate purr making Tavias's cock strain against the confines of his leather britches. Tavias rubbed a circle around her belly, calming her just a hair's breadth. No more. He'd told her the state he intended to bring her too, and he'd been honest at that.

"Now you must *really* not move," he said. "Not even twitch a muscle. Least we singe something I will regret."

He set the fire alight between Kit's open thighs, all his concentration on the tiny flame. It was hot and close enough to her folds, her clit, that she'd feel the heat intensely on her most sensitive parts. But there was moisture there too now. And there was Tavias's control that he stretched to its fullest as he made the wine burn bright, bright, brighter.

Tavias made himself breath as he feasted on the vision of her bound by flame and displayed before him like an offering to the gods. She was exquisite in her vulnerability, trembling with a mix of fear and desire as she awaited his next move. Yes, she was all his now. The scent of her arousal intensified with each moment, mixing with the heady perfume of the wine.

Letting the flames go out, Tavias took his time shifting the few stray strands of hair that fluttered onto Kit's face. Each time he touched her, he trailed his fingers over her skin. Her pulse. The connection between them was starting to thrum, as if it had its own magic and pulse.

Without taking his attention from her, Tavias picked up the candle, channeling his magic to ensure the wick burned high and bright within Kit's line of sight. He moved slowly, but offered neither warning nor explanation as he tilted it, letting the hot wax drip onto Kit's breast.

She arched at the scalding heat, a short pitiful sound coming from her throat. But the moment of pain was as short lived as Tavias knew it would be. The wax hardened, contracting around the contours of her areola in a way that made the sound coming from her change to one of sharp arousal. The scent of beeswax filled the air, rich and earthy and coalescing with the growing arousal.

Kit's and Tavias's. Stars. His cock was getting so hard that it hurt.

The once panicked look in Kit's eyes turned to desperation, her body now twitching with unanswered need. She'd not be able to hold this position much longer. Tavias dripped more wax on her, creating swirling patterns across her flesh until she trembled outright. He traced a finger through the wax and her hips undulated, trying to ride the air.

Making his choice carefully, Tavias finally peeled away a strip of wax around the mating bite Quinton left on Kit's breast. The skin beneath was pink and sensitive. Leaning down, he licked at the revealed flesh, his tongue flicking over her bunched nipple in a tease that had her moaning unabashedly.

"Please," she pleaded. "Please, it hurts."

Tavias put his hand between her folds, letting her know that he knew exactly which ache she complained of. She was dripping wet now, nothing like before. That was good. Because this couldn't end just yet, not for the type of submission the priests would expect to see.

Another broken whimper came from her. "Please, I need..."

"I know exactly what you think you need." He slid his head down, nudging her thighs apart even farther to bare the glistening folds between. Dipping his head, he licked a broad stroke through her sex, growling at the taste of her arousal.

Kit jerked, a strangled cry on her lips. He speared his tongue into her entrance, thrusting deep as he sought the sensitive spot within. When he found it, Kit screamed, back arching off the table.

Tavias pulled back an instant before she could find completion. Which was, admittedly, cruel. But this game wasn't for her pleasure, it was for her life.

That denial made Kit's control over herself shatter completely. Her wax-speckled body writhed on the table, desire burning in her every desperate twitch. She reached for him, gripping his arms.

Tavias caught her wrists, forcing them down. "I do not recall granting permission to move," he said, his voice hard as stone.

Kit blinked. Her eyes were so glazed with need that she was having trouble focusing. Understanding.

"Now, I'm going to punish you for disobeying me," Tavias clarified for her benefit. He put extra emphasis on the word *punish*, letting all the velvet promise and threat come together in two short syllables.

With a firm grip, he lifted Kit up. Her body was warm and supple in his hands, her dyed blond hair cascading down her back. As he bent her over the table, the sight of her full backside and dragon tattoo made his own breath quicken. Stars, this was supposed to be torment for her, not him.

With Kit folded over the table, Tavias spared one look at the priests. If not for them, he'd have Kit savoring her pleasure three times over by now. Instead, he returned to tormenting the delicious little wildcat spread before him.

Tavias stroked Kit's backside once, then parted it, feeling the heat emanating from her. He slid his fingers between her thighs, gathering her slickness to use as lubricant.

The realization of what was about to happen dawned on Kit a few seconds later than it usually would, her body tensing and clenching in defiance. She tried to squirm out of the way, but Tavias held her firmly in place, spurring arousal and embarrassment both. It was always thus with Kit. Her body liked being taken from the back. Her mind hated her enjoyment of it.

Tavias pressed Kit down more firmly against the table, his large hand splayed across her lower back. With little ceremony about it, he delivered a pair of stinging swats. She inhaled sharply, her flesh flushing a light pink that made her squirm in equal parts pain and pleasure. Before she could recover from the sensation, he slid his fingers between her slick folds and stroked her channel before pulling out. The ring of another spank echoed through the hall, the wetness on Tavias's hand amplifying the sound.

He continued in the same vein, juxtaposing sting and pleasure until Kit's whole body shook with need. Each time his fingers brushed against her clit, a surge of energy seemed to race up her spine, leaving her breathless and wanting more.

Stars, she was beautiful. Responsive. Brave and trusting against all odds.

Pulling open his flies, Tavias allowed his bulging erection to spring free. The column of scales along his cock bristled before laying tight and flat in preparation. This time, Kit offered no resistance when he positioned himself at her back entrance, his fingers still pumping in and out of her channel as he pushed himself inside.

CHAPTER 22

Kit

*M*y core pulses with need as I lay bent over the table, my body Tavias's for the taking. The cool wood presses against my bare stomach, providing a stark contrast to the heat emanating from Tavias behind me. His fingers circle my hips, pulling me closer with each powerful thrust that sends shivers down my spine He fills me completely, the stretch and burn morphing to sinful pleasure.

It's so wrong. But so right too.

I take in a sharp breath, feeling his hand slip around me and into my folds, teasing the sensitive bundle of nerves. The sensation is overwhelming. The room flutters and spins around me until only Tavias's relentless pounding fills my awareness. Each time his hips connect with mine, a new shiver of sensation runs down my spine. My breaths come in short, ragged gasps, mingling with the husky grunts escaping Tavias' lips. I press into him, trying to get more.

My nails dig into the wooden table, desperate for something to hold onto as I teeter on the brink of orgasm.

Suddenly, Tavias slows his pace, gripping my hips as he pivots me away from the table. Confusion and frustration flood through me until I catch sight of what Tavias is turning me toward. Cyril, Hauck, and Quinton prowl toward us, each wearing expressions of primal hunger. The scales along their temples rise and the very air around them seems to vibrate with energy.

A surge of heat envelops me as Cyril takes his place in front, his firm chest pressing against my heaving bosom. Tavias doesn't relent; instead, his grip on my hips grows tighter, and I can feel him continuing to push into me from behind even as Cyril lifts my slick thighs. He pushes into me and the double sensation, the fullness of it, is overwhelming. And then they start moving.

In all our escapades, the males have not taken me like this before. A whimper escapes me. Each thrust of the males' cocks inside me magnifies the other. And their scales... stars. They come to life inside my channels, seeking each spot of pleasure until I'm shaking.

Hauck's hands find my breasts, the pads of his fingers teasing yet gentle as they trace delicate patterns around my nipples. He lifts one breast, weighing it in his hand before giving it an enticing squeeze. My body shudders in response, my muscles under their control more than mine.

Even the scents swirling around me are intoxicating—the musky scent of male arousal, the tangy aroma of sweat mingling with the softer notes of my own arousal. I taste the saltiness of my own perspiration on my lips, and the air is thick with the sounds of our heavy breathing, moans, and the slickness of our bodies moving together.

I cry out, but Quinton's mouth is suddenly there, swallowing the sound. His kiss is deep and claiming, and for a heartbeat the taste of him fills my awareness completely. I try to respond in kind, but his tongue pillages my mouth, taking utter control. The bond between us preens.

My body is trembling now, caught in the throes of my growing need. Tavias's powerful thrusts send shockwaves through me, their intensity amplified by the firm pressure of Cyril pressing against my front. Hauck's skilled fingers continue to toy with my nipples, each twist and tweak sending sparks of sensation arcing through me. Every nerve ending is alive, every stroke and suckle and shift of scales lifting me higher and higher above the chasm of impending release.

The same release that Tavias has denied me so many times already.

I whimper pitifully against Quinton's mouth.

"Please. Please, it hurts. Please." My words sound like sobs as I writhe beneath the males' relentless ministrations. "Please. I can't—Tavias!"

"Just a little more, wildcat." Tavias's voice is a low growl that sets my heart racing even faster. I can't take any more. I can't. The abyss opening beneath me is already too great. The need too overpowering. I can't wait another moment.

But I don't have a choice. Not with the control the males have on me. On my pleasure.

"Now," says Tavias.

Teeth scrape over my neck and nick my flesh. A mouth suckles my nipple. And an amber burst of flame licks my clit.

I shriek my release, convulsing so hard that my body is a white-hot wave of ecstasy and torment. The males growl around me, a crescendo that echoes my own. They find their release an instant later. Everywhere inside me. On me. All together as one.

My body goes limp, completely spent and utterly exhausted as the tidal wave of pleasure slowly ebbs away. Tavias holds me as he pulls out, Cyril checking my balance from the other side. They have to. I'm as weak and trembling as a newborn kitten. Utterly destroyed. Just as Tavias had promised.

The hall slowly comes into focus. Guests in elegant gowns. Servants with food. Priests with their hoods and judgmental eyes. I sink to the floor, dimly aware of the priests conferring amongst themselves in hushed tones, their eyes never straying far from my vulnerable naked form. The males make no move to cover me. I know they can't. I remember why this happened.

Keep your head down, little wildcat, Tavias urges inside my mind. *We are all here. You were brave. Exquisite. Generous. We all know it, even if we can't show it just now. Not just yet.*

The priests' conference concludes. My stomach sinks.

"Have your requirements been satisfied, my priest?" Tavias bows low.

I hate that he is bowing for the order. For the damn priests.

"It was never *my* requirement, Tavias," the head priest declares, his tone solemn, "but the Goddess Orion's test."

"Of course." Tavias bows again. I know the priest is just milking this now and my hatred for him grows several notches.

He inhales dramatically. "Yes. I can see the human has been brought to heel. I advise you to keep her there, as the Goddess shall not be so generous in the future."

Tavias goes to the priests to express gratitude that I can't bear to listen to while Hauck's strong arms encircle me, lifting me gently off the cold stone floor. His warmth seeps into my trembling flesh as he cradles me against his chest. As he carries me to the sidelines, I become acutely aware of the dozens of eyes that bore into us still. Geoffrey's and Bianca's and Ettienne's. Everyone who saw me lose all control, be swatted and taken, and driven to beg for release.

Heat fills my face. But there's nowhere to hide, nothing to do but endure the stares as I try to regain some semblance of control over my shattered body and scattered thoughts.

"You are gorgeous when you come," Hauck says, nipping

my ear. "The moment we walk free of this pit, I want to see how many new ways I can conjure up to bring you pleasure."

I know he means well—hell, he probably means every word—but I can't bring myself to respond. He shifts me on his lap, and then Cyril is there with a wet cloth to wipe my skin.

"I know you enjoyed that," Cyril says with a hint of a smile. "Bloody stars, I think the whole kingdom knows it. And we enjoyed it no less intensely."

I turn my face. I did enjoy it. And isn't that the whole problem? That I lost control of everything and begged for mindless pleasure like the animal the priests make the humans to be?

"She is dropping," Hauck says over my head. I don't know what that means but concern flickers over Cyril's face even as he strokes a knuckle along my cheekbone.

Quinton appears at my side, a glass of water in hand. "Drink, human."

"I'd rather have wine," I say. Around us, the hall is slowly turning to a cacophony of moans and cries as other packs remember the priest's initial orders and hurry to prove their humans compatible. The air is thick with lust and sweat, and the sounds of flesh against flesh echoing through the room.

"No." Quinton presses the water to my lips. "Drink the water."

I do, not realizing how badly I needed the cool liquid until it trickles down my parched throat.

With tender hands, Hauck begins to dress me, carefully

sliding my clothes back into place. His deftness with the chest binding and dress straps speak of experience I've always known he's had. The soft fabric brushes against my hypersensitive skin, reigniting sparks of sensation that sends shudders down my spine. I can't meet anyone's gaze.

I hear it then. The call of the familiar song that pulls me toward it. The musicians are long gone and nothing about the male's faces suggest that they note anything strange. I draw in a breath and use Hauck's muscled shoulder to climb to my feet. I want my body back. My control of it.

Cyril moves to spot me immediately, but Quinton meets my gaze and holds his brother back.

"She can stand," he says with curt finality. "She is one of our pack, not a doll."

That's… Somehow that's the best thing I've ever heard. Not that I say that aloud. Instead, I clear my throat. "Do you hear that?" I ask. "The music. A song. Slow, like a lullaby."

Quinton's mouth tightens, Hauck and Cyril exchanging glances.

Clearly, they do not.

I shake my head. "Alright, so maybe I'm not all together in my right mind yet."

Hauck extends his hand, beckoning me back toward him. "My pride would be irreparably wounded if after all that you got your mind back so quickly. Come soothe my fragile ego and pretend you need me a bit longer?"

"Actually, I'm going to use the privy."

"I'll take you," Cyril offers.

"No." I realize my voice has risen and check it quickly. "Please," I raise my palms. "Just let me do something on my own. Using the privy isn't a group experience."

The males exchange glances, clearly reluctant to let me out of their sight. Cyril relents finally, his shoulders heaving with a long exhale. "We'll be waiting for you."

"Great." I say as I back away from them and toward that soul-pulling music.

CHAPTER 23

Kit

The music pulls me. A familiar song from a time I don't remember. As if excited by my acknowledgement of it, the music gets more intense the closer I get to the tapestry covered side exit that leads toward the privy. The sound is not just in my ears, but in my skin. On the inside of my forearm.

I watch the faces around me, trying to see if anybody else hears the sound. They don't seem to. Or are too busy rutting to notice. Not even the priests who are congregated on the dais, their hoods over their heads as always. It makes me wonder what their hair is like. Maybe they are bald under all that fabric. I hope the assholes are bald and can't grow their hair no matter how badly they wish to.

The music seems to beckon me and me alone. Which is a really good reason to not go investigating, even though I desperately need to do something alone right now. Still, I should swallow what's left of my shredded pride and go back.

I start to.

A pain sharp enough to take my breath lances through my forearm. The music increases. There is a desperation to it now, a fear and plea that I can't refuse. I duck through the hanging tapestry into a decorated foyer, and am surprised when the next tapestry I bump into likewise gives way. Stepping through it, I find myself in a narrow stone corridor lit by sparse torches. From here I see the spot from which I entered. It's so narrow that my having bumped the tapestry at that particular point is no way a coincidence.

The music pulls me along, the phantomly familiar tune in my head coalescing into words.

In the heart of the ancient skies,
Where stars shimmer and fire flies,
Lay a dragon, wings spread wide,
Whispering secrets of the tide.
Close your eyes, little ember's glow,
Let the winds of dreams softly blow,
To realms beyond, where dragons fly,
Sailing the canvas of the sky.

A lullaby. I couldn't have heard it before, and yet I know the next verse.

Breathe in deep, the night's embrace,

Feel the stars kiss your fiery face,

For in dreams, all dragons are free,

To soar, to dance, to simply be.

I realize I'm singing along with the strange siren as I follow its call down the corridor, which spills into a larger, wider one before dividing and pulling off again, taking me to the bowels of the citadel. I hurry, knowing that I can't be gone long. The music guides me through several more turns before depositing me by a door.

The very air around me vibrates and the lullaby starts from the beginning. Knowing that what I'm about to do falls under bad life choices, I push against the door handle.

It's locked.

Of course it's locked. Why wouldn't it be? The song stops and I realize how stupid this whole thing is. I give the door one final tug just to make sure and—

It opens.

My heart jumps. The music restarts, coming from the other side of the door. My forearm burns. I can't help myself, or maybe I can and I'm just choosing not to. I go inside.

Warm moist air surrounds me as I enter the room, a stark contrast to the cool corridor I'd just left. The space unfolds as a circular chamber, its walls painted with a soft iridescent sheen, reflecting colors that dance like the northern lights. There is an earthy scent of moist soil and flowers, which is probably coming from the vats of greenery set up all around the room's periphery. The flowering plants stretch tall toward the sunbeams filtering in from skylights overhead. Is this where the flowers for the fertility elixir grow? No. Of course not. That would make no sense.

The makeshift greenhouses are not the real heart of the room though. All my attention centers on a very large ornately decorated wooden crate in the chamber's center. The crate's wood is dark, almost black, and etched with runes—the biggest one being two overlapping circles. Sibling to the brand on my arm.

The music, the pull, its coming from inside the crate. I feel it vibrating along my skin and settle on my tongue with a tangy sweetness. My breath is still as I step closer—only to find the crate sealed from all sides. There is no lid to open. But there is something inside. Something that's making my heart sync to the *lub dub, lub dub, lub dub* of its rhythm.

As I run my hand along the crate's wood, the lullaby rekindles in my soul. There is a different feel to it now. It's happy to see me. Desperate. Welcoming.

"What are you?" I whisper to the crate.

There is no answer. I circle around it several times, finally finding a small crack through which I can glance inside. I don't know what I expect to see—possibly a creature of some kind. Instead, I see pebbled sides of five giant eggs. The eggs — if that's what they are — seemed to shift ever so slightly, their colors morphing and blending.

Stars.

My hand slides across the crate, accidentally brushing one of the circle-overlapping runes. That sends a sharp jolt running up my arm, forcing me to pull back instantly. As if the crate is guarding its contents, warding off intruders.

The jolt also snaps me back to reality. I've no business in this room, nothing to even say if I get caught here. Not to mention that I've been gone too long from the celestial hall already. Whatever this is about, I need the pack and Autumn to unravel it.

The eggs seem to sense my intention and send that lullaby into my head again. Promising that I'd return when I can, I carefully open the door a crack and ensure the dimly lit corridor beyond it is empty before stepping out. Outside the room, the cold hits me all at once, the oppression of the citadel descending on me. Shadows dance along the walls as I make my way back toward the ballroom, the flickering torchlight casting an unwelcoming glow on the stone.

I keep myself close to the wall, using the shadows to mask my movements. Ironically, I'm following the sounds again— though this time I'm heading toward the shrieks and grunts of the celestial hall. At least some of the packs must still be in the middle of proving their compatibility to the priests.

I'm nearly back when the sound of footsteps stops me in my tracks, sending a jolt of fear down my spine. There is no time to react before a figure steps around the corner, his face shadowed by the hood of a priest of Orion.

Blood drains from my face.

"What are you doing here?" the priest demands, blocking my path. I don't recognize him but I'm sure he knows who I am. Hell, I'm pretty sure every mouse in the citadel knows who I am now.

I drop my head, my heart hammering so fiercely that the rushing blood makes me dizzy.

"I was looking for the privy," I stammer into my feet. "Might you point me down the right path?"

The priest weighs me with his attention, which is as penetrating as any look Quinton gives. A fresh tremor of fears runs through me, but at least this part makes sense—any human would be terrified in my shoes. I press my knees together and give the priest the most pitiful expression I can muster, "Please, your grace? I really need to relieve myself and I've gotten myself turned around."

The priest's cold assessment gives me no window into his thoughts. Just as I'm certain he's seen through my ruse however, he nods once. "Follow me."

"Thank you," I manage to choke out, following him the short distance to the privy chamber.

"I will await you here," the man says, stopping outside the privy door.

I briefly consider whether telling him that is unnecessary would more likely hurt or help me, and settle on bowing and keeping my mouth shut. Going inside the privy, I do my business quickly and take another moment to splash some water over my face. As I gaze at my reflection in the small mirror above the wash basin, a mix of determination and desperation stares back at me. Determination and desperation in a purple chiffon dress.

The priest is still there as he promised when I come out. He offers a curt nod, and we begin our journey back to the celestial hall. With each step, my senses sharpen, anxiety gnawing at the edges of my thoughts. Something about that room, that *nest* feels wrong on a visceral level. Something about this entire setup feels wrong, no matter how much Cyril and the others insist that the trial competitions are the least of all evils, a way of keeping the peace.

As we near the entrance, I see not much time has passed since my departure, at least not in the activity sense. Dragon shifters and humans are still going at each other while guests watch, the scents of arousal and wine heavy in the air. Lee is among those who have finished already. She at least looks thoroughly satisfied, her skin a glowing blush.

All four of my males stalk toward me the moment I enter the celestial hall, and they are the most wonderful sight I've ever beheld. Even if they are furious. After what I just saw, I don't care if they yell at me or hold me or anything in between, so long as they listen. And I know they will. They are my pack.

"Come with me." The priest's hand closes on my upper arm, catching me before I can get to the males. With a firm grip, the priest directs me toward the front of the hall, where the other priests keep watch from their dais. Murmurs spread throughout the room like wildfire, and I can feel the weight of countless eyes upon me again. At least the eyes of those not currently in the middle of a rut.

"Kneel," the priest who'd led me here commands, his tone

leaving no room for argument. "It seems here is the safest place for you this evening."

I obey, dropping to my knees, frustration boiling my blood. My males stop a few paces away, another priest blocking their path with an outstretched staff. Behind me, my priest speaks with those in charge, but the voices are too low to hear.

Are you hurt? Tavias's voice sounds in my head, nearly making me jump. *Tap your right knee for yes, left for no.*

I swallow and tap my left knee. *No.*

Is everything alright?

That's one loaded question. But I only have two choices for an answer, so I go with the most true one. Left knee. *No.*

Tavias's spine stiffens. I know that he wants to keep this interrogation going, but we can talk like normal people later. What I really need is for someone—for Quinton—to talk to Autumn while there is a chance. To find more information on what she thinks about the brand. I try to signal as much to Quinton, cutting my gaze between him and the petite princess who is still near the dessert table.

A sigh of relief leaves me when he wanders away from the pack, but I know better than to bring any attention to him and Autumn. From the way Tavias introduced me and her earlier, I'm certain no one but me knows about the arrangement she and Quinton have.

Kit. Kitterny.

I realize Tavias is talking to me again. From the sound of

it, he's been trying to get my attention for some time. I lower my head in apology to him. I know he's worried about me.

Are you alright? Tavias asks.

I tap my right knee. *Yes.*

He frowns. *You are alright, but everything is not alright?*

Yes.

Explaining something as complicated as finding a secret room with a crate of singing eggs and mini greenhouses of plants that might be for the fertility elixir is just not something that easy to do with this conversation set up.

Like a symbol of shame, the priests leave me to kneel on the hard floor for the next two hours, while the celebration comes to a too slow close. For the first time since coming to the trial grounds, I'm actually glad to hear the sound of the gong.

"May I have everyone's attention," the head priest calls, while all the lights of the celestial hall—with the exception of the few surrounding the dais—dim. Having thus captured everyone's attention, the priest once again goes into his sermon about the power of the goddess, and the sacred rite, and the general importance of the priests of Orion in keeping the world from descending into chaos. As he makes an extra detour to remind everyone that the dragons are surviving at all only due to the priests' efforts with the elixir, it occurs to me that the dragons aren't the only ones to benefit from this potion of mystical power.

The priests are making out very well too, with even the

king of Massa'eve being forced here to pay his respects and play their games.

There is some editorial genuflecting on the part of the crowd, but nothing about this set up feels benevolent to me anymore. Especially not after tonight. I close my eyes, counting down the seconds before the bloody priest dismisses us and I can tell the males what I found. It all means something. I know in my gut that it does.

"Before we release the packs," the priest says, "we have a change of schedule to announce. This rite has been difficult already and—while it is our duty to find the pack most worthy to carry on the dragon bloodline—we do not wish to stretch the ordeal out longer than we must. As such, we have moved up the second trial. Instead of waiting another week as planned, the trial shall begin... now."

CHAPTER 24

Kit

*M*y head snaps up. What does he mean now? As in *now*, now?

That doesn't work for me. Not one bit. I scramble up to my feet and rush toward Tavias and the pack, but a priest's staff blocks my path. At once, two more priests appear beside me, each grabbing hold of my arms. They aren't letting me get to the males.

Save your strength, wildcat, Tavias commands into my mind. *You won't win the fight just now.*

It takes all my willpower to keep from fighting the two priests holding me, but Tavias is right. No good can come of a struggle just now. More priests pour into the celestial hall, separating out the humans. Some of the women are so unsteady on their feet from the wine and the rutting that they must be held up lest they fall.

"In the first trial, Orion tested the worthiness of the humans," the high priest continues, ignoring the rising chorus of whispers and soft gasps. It's not the description of the first trial that I'd have offered, but no one is asking my opinion. The priest raises his voice dramatically. "For the second trial, she shall test the resolve of the dragons."

This declaration gets a cheer from guests and competitors alike.

"The rules are straight forward," the priest continues once the shouts settle. "Over the next three hours, the humans will be scattered throughout the trial grounds. Each packs must simply locate the women and keep them alive for a week."

A small murmur ripples over the hall as everyone likely reads between the same lines I do. Nothing in the rules prohibits packs from killing or taking other packs' women, and with the entire trial grounds at play, it's anyone's guess who will find who first. This is going to be a hunt. And a bloody one.

I really wish my mind connection with Tavias worked both ways.

Don't look for us, Tavias says quickly. *Head for high ground if you can. Hide. Your job is to stay alive. Leave the tracking to us.*

I nod. It's as much of a plan as we are going to get. At least I'm in better shape than some of the girls. I feel Quinton's gaze along with the pull of our bond. He is strung as tight as a bow string. All the males are.

"With my life," Quinton mouths to me. An echo of what he'd said when we were bonded. Hauck and Cyril's eyes make the same promise. I long to go to them, to throw my arms around the pack one more time, but the priests' hold is so tight that I can't.

"One week," the priest adds with a final flourish. "One week to survive the Goddess's challenge. One week to protect the bride to be. One week until we all gather here again to discover which packs are worthy of the precious elixir. At that time too, the third and final trial shall be announced. We shall see you all then."

I don't look back at the pack as the priests lead me and the other women into a separate chamber. There are twelve stools set out here, each holding a neat pile of clothes. We each get thick leggings, a woolen dress, boots and a fur lined cloak that seems overkill for the nippy, but not severe, weather outside. Lee and I help the few girls who can't seem to manage changing on their own.

There is also a satchel of food and a canteen beside each stool. Bianca, of course, tries to take two for herself but backs down when several of the women come to stand beside me and Lee. It's a small victory, but it feels important. Especially because the priests seem unhappy about it. They want us to fight even while they claim to want order. I'm getting a sense there are a lot of mismatches between what the priests claim and what they want.

In the heart of the ancient skies,
Where stars shimmer and fire flies,

Lay a dragon, wings spread wide,
Whispering secrets of the tide.

THE WORDS of the phantom lullaby start playing in my head again. I shove them down along with the memories of the circular chamber. There will be time to deal with that later. For now, I have to do as Tavias asked. I have to stay alive.

With everyone changed, the priests start leading the women away one at a time.

I grab Lee's hand, which is cold with fear despite all the warm clothing, and lean close to her ear.

"If you can move safely, head towards the highest ground on the trials' field," I whisper, giving her a description of where we set up camp. My pack is stronger than Lee's and others may think twice about attacking her there. It feels good to be in control of something, even just of directing a friend to safety. "My males won't harm you, I promise. I'll meet you there."

"Maybe we'll find each other on the way," Lee says, shuddering as the priests head for her. "I'll look for you."

"As will I." I conjure a brave smile for her benefit. "I'll see you soon."

I watch Lee be led away, then Bianca, then the others, until I am the last one left in the room. I stand next to the door, waiting for my turn and trying to feel as brave as I made myself seem. My pack is the strongest of the dragons out there. They will be fine. We all will be.

Footsteps approach on the other side of the door, then stop. "She is in there alone?" the head priest's familiar voice asks. "Have we learned any more, Juan?"

"No sir." I recognize the voice of the priest who'd found me in the corridor. "If you have concerns, why not remove her now and be done with it?"

My breathing halts and I press myself against the wall.

"One of the idiot princes bonded her. He will know when she ends." The head priest sounds put out. "With all the eyes on the royal pack, there should be nothing to suggest irregularity."

That's good. I think that's good.

"Especially when it's simple enough to get distance," the priest adds. "Let's have a chat with the wench first."

The door knob turns and I scurry to the other side of the room. By the time the priests come in, I'm crouching in the corner and wishing I still had my knife. Not that I could take three males out with one blade. My heart pounds, my mouth too dry to swallow.

"Lady Kitterny." The head priest closes the door behind him and gives me a cold smile. "What a pleasure to finally meet you."

Juan and his partner grab my elbows, and haul me to kneel at the head priest's feet. I crane my neck up to look at him. My mind spins to decipher what he might want. "I believe we've met, your grace."

"Not in so private a setting though." He tilts his head, then picks up a strand of my blond-dyed hair and rubs it between his fingers. His brow arches. "Interesting. Tell me, who are your parents?"

"Lord and Lady Agam, your grace. They own the Agam estate."

"It is unwise to lie to me," the priest says.

Juan raises a hand to strike me.

"No," the priest interrupts. "Do not leave marks."

Juan lowers his hand, but glares at me.

The high priest sighs. "The Agams are not your birth parents." He sounds certain. "Tell me who your birth parents are."

"I never met my father and my mother died when I was little. The Agams raised me."

The high priest steps closer and there is a note of gravity in his low voice. "Tell me about your mother."

"I don't remember her, your grace."

"Try."

I scrunch my face for a few seconds before shaking my head in apology that convinces absolutely no one. Since I'm pretty certain the priests intend to kill me, I'm not sure how much it matters though.

The head priest sighs. "The priests of Orion are protectors, Kitterny. We save lives. Do you not wish to help?"

I don't know where to even start unpacking that statement, so I just bow my head.

"The time, your grace," Juan warns the priest.

The high priest shakes his head in disappointment then takes a vile out of the folds of his robe. The vibrant orange color of the liquid inside reminds me of one of the flower types I saw in the circular room.

"It's called a Bloody Sunset," the head priest explains as the others tighten their hold. "It is a paralytic. Very difficult to make but there is no antidote and even a small dose will incapacitate a dragon. For a human, I fear there is no chance of recovery at all." The priest uncorks the bottle, unleashing a sickly sweet scent into the air.

Juan grabs my jaw, his fingers digging in painfully to force my mouth open. Terror rushes through me, my thudding heart racing with my thoughts. The head priest steps closer, bottle in hand. My stomach churns.

"Don't fight," Juan warns.

Like hell I won't. I shift my weight, planting one foot firmly behind me. Pushing off, I launch myself forward. The priest holding me curses, losing his grip, and I feel the satisfying thud of my shoulder connecting with Juan's knee.

The contact is sharp, solid.

Jaun lets out a shout of pain. Stumbles. He isn't at all like my pack. He's weak. Untrained. Using the momentary distraction, I swing my elbow backward into the stomach of the other priest. He grunts.

I jump to my feet, my attention focusing on the door. My only escape. I dash for it.

Arms grab me from behind, lifting me off the floor before slamming me down hard. The impact makes my knees scream. The priest behind me wrenches my arms back so hard that I can feel my shoulders tearing.

A scream escapes me.

Jaun, who'd fallen, pulls himself back to his feet. His lips are peeled in a snarl, his nostrils flaring, his precious hood knocked off his head.

Through my haze of pain, I slowly register what I see. His ears. His rounded human ears.

"You... you are mortal," I grunt.

"No. We are not." The head priest grabs my jaw and forces my mouth open. He moves swiftly this time, pouring the orange potion down my throat before I can stop him. My head is pulled back, forcing me to swallow or choke. No matter how much I fight, the sickly sweetness coats my mouth, my tongue, my throat, burning as it goes down.

For a moment, nothing happens. But then a cold, creeping numbness snakes from the pit of my stomach outward, stealing warmth and sensation as it goes. My heart continues to race, yet it feels muffled, as if smothered by layers of dense cotton. My limbs grow heavy, a dead weight I cannot move at all. My tongue, too, becomes thick and unyielding, falling lifelessly against my mouth.

Panic surges, yet I can't express it. I can't scream. Can't move. My lungs are the only refuge from the potion's paralyzing grip, but the shallow breaths they draw on their own are no longer in my control. Everything I could once move is now hostage to the potion' grip.

Desperate thoughts scream within the confines of my mind, begging my fingers to twitch, my eyelids to blink, anything to prove I'm not entirely trapped in this motionless cage. But the potion is thorough, its hold on me unrelenting.

"Hike her a few miles from the citadel," the head priest instructs. "Make it look good."

I can do nothing as I'm lifted and carried outside into a blazing winter storm. I've no notion how the priests managed to transform the entire Equinox Trials' grounds into the dead of winter, but they did. The howling winds sound like wailing spirits, and each gust feels like a thousand icy needles pricking my exposed skin.

Snowflakes, vast and chunky, cascade down in relentless torrents, obliterating all signs of landmarks and pathways. I can barely see the length of my own hand through the curtains of snow and the priests' footprints disappear in seconds. I can't look up to the sky, but the lack of dragon roars tells me that the packs are being held back for now. That no one is around to witness this.

My captors move with methodical precision, each step deliberate against the deepening snowdrifts. After what feels like an eternity, the priests stop and lower me to the ground. They're careful in their cruelty, adjusting my limbs just so. My left foot is twisted at an odd angle, caught in a raised bank of snow as if I had stumbled over it. My right arm is splayed outward while my left arm is tucked under my torso, creating the illusion of a fall. My head is slightly turned, half-buried in the snow, mouth and nose nearly covered, as if I had tried to lift it, but failed.

I want to scream, but the paralytic holds me firm.

"How long, do you think?" Juan asks.

"She will never move again, but she will remain alive until her body freezes." The priest makes a contemplative sound. "In this weather, a day at the most. Less."

"I feel... unsettled."

"It is a necessary sacrifice." He sighs. "We can make it go faster for her."

I hear something scraping. The sound is familiar and I realize it's the rasp of a canteen being opened. Then... Water pours over me, soaking my dress. The wet fabric makes the cold suddenly a thousand times worse. Ten thousand times. My lungs seize. I can barely breathe. Or shiver. Or scream.

One of the priests leans down to close my eyes for me, before the pair walks away.

CHAPTER 25

Quinton

"Over here!" Quinton's holler barely pierced the howling gale to reach the others. His breath hung in the air, a cloud of vapor that was quickly swept away by the relentless gusts. The once crisp and mild autumn air had been replaced by a harsh, unnatural winter snowstorm that swept mercilessly across the mountainous forest. Quinton had no idea how the priests managed it. Nor did he care. He cared about nothing but one thing.

His mate.

His fierce, fragile, mortal mate who'd been out in the elements for six hours. She was still alive. Quinton knew that because he was still alive, but that was of little consolation. Quinton was fading. Stumbling over his own feet.

When the trial was announced, Quinton had readied himself to fight every dragon at the citadel. He was good at fighting. Good at killing. But the priests had twisted things again. Quinton's teeth and claws and wings did no good against the cold.

"You felt her again?" Tavias trudged up beside Quinton.

With the poor visibility, they'd given up searching from the sky hours ago, leaning instead into the pull of Quinton's mating bond. When the trial started, the flares of pain and sheer panic the bond carried to him had sent him into fits of rage. That was before he learned how much more frightening silence was. And the bond had been dead silent for the past half an hour. Until now.

"Yes." Quinton closed his eyes, focusing on the bond that connected him to Kit. It was faint, a mere thread amidst the cacophony of the storm, but it was there, a beacon guiding him towards... toward here. This spot. "She is here. *Here*."

Here was nothing but a blanket of deep clean snow. Dropping to his knees, Quinton started to dig, his brothers following his lead without question. Quinton's breath came in ragged gasps, his lungs aching from the frigid air. The snowstorm raged around them, swallowing every sound and obscuring their vision. His nostrils flared, attempting to catch even the faintest scent of Kit, but the biting wind tore at his senses, making it near impossible.

The unmistakable jolt of connection surged through Quinton again. Here. She was here.

"I have her," Hauck roared.

The pack converged on Hauck's spot, everyone's frostbitten faces etched with the same mixture of hope and dread that pounded through Quinton as they pushed snow aside with their hands.

Kit was unconscious. Unmoving. The snow surrounding her body was densely packed, a sign she'd been there for a while. Her right arm was spread outward, fingers peeking through the white blanket, while her left was tucked under her body. Her clothes, soaked from melted snow and then frozen again, clung to her body, making her appear like a statue. From the way her left foot was twisted, as if she'd caught it on something, Kit appeared to have fallen.

Quinton ran his fingers over her face. It was slightly turned to the side, melting snow trickling down her pale cheeks and full blue lips.

Hauck lifted her into his arms, which was fair since it was he who'd first found her.

"Hey, turnip," he called. "Time to wake up."

No response. Not even a blink or change in the rhythm of her breath. But the mating bond still pulsed between them, weak but unmistakable. It was a lifeline, a connection that tethered her to this world. Quinton would do everything in his power to keep it from breaking.

They carried her up to their camp, Cyril and Tavias taking charge of security while Quinton and Hauck stayed with Kit. Quinton's stomach clenched into a knot. He couldn't shake the feeling that, despite having been found,

Kit's time was running out. That she slipped further away with every moment.

Once at camp, the pack's entire focus turned to re-warming the mortal. Hauck peeled the frozen garments from Kit's body, the pieces coming away in solid blocks, each holding the cold that had nearly killed her.

Quinton didn't remember discarding his own clothes, but the moment Kit was naked, so was he. He gathered her against him, the chill of her skin jarring against his warmth. A moment later, Hauck was equally naked on Kit's other side, the pair of them pouring every ounce of warmth into her.

Cyril hauled in several large stones from the outside, Tavias channeling his magic into the rocks. The heated stones hissed and steamed, creating a barrier against the relentless chill until the whole shelter felt like a greenhouse amidst a winter storm. Quinton felt the heat from Tavias's magic and his brothers' bodies working together, the warmth slowly seeping into Kit's icy form. The once-loud wind outside became a distant hum, overshadowed by the thick silence inside.

Hours passed. Kit's limbs warmed, her skin regaining a pinkish glow that Quinton was used to seeing. But still, she did not open her eyes and the mating bond continued to whine with a low steady hum of despair. Unable to sit still, Quinton paced the length of their shelter, stopping every few steps to listen for any sounds of an approaching assault. They were vulnerable now. His mate was vulnerable.

"She is fine," Tavias announced, crossing his arms. His voice was edged with a promise of violence to anyone who dared disagree and the clothes he'd put back on shifted over coiling muscles. "She is exhausted. Pushed beyond her limit. Of course she is asleep."

Hauck, who was taking his turn cradling Kit against him, brushed a strand of hair from her face. "Fight it turnip," he whispered. "We've some flying to do, you and I. Think of all the people we've not pissed off yet. Hardly seems right to stop now. Open your eyes just for a moment, and I promise I'll fly you anywhere you want. We can perch on the tallest spire of the citadel or else shoot through the clouds. Maybe not during the winter, but you'll love that on a hot day. Blink just once, and we have a bargain."

Quinton continued pacing, his steps soft against the ground. Kit was alive. She was *there*. He could feel her essence through their bond. And yet she showed no sign of it. "This isn't right," stopping suddenly. "It doesn't add up."

"She lay frozen in the snow," Tavias's magic danced over his scales, his temper rising. "She just needs time. That's why the priests gave us a week."

"She might be poisoned," Cyril said.

"Then she'd be dead," Tavias snapped.

"Not all poisons kill," said Quinton.

"You'd know, wouldn't you." Tavias grabbed the front of Quinton's shirt, twisting it. He wanted to fight. Needed to. Quinton understood. "What's the poison in her, Shadow? Where do we find the antidote? Tell me."

"Her pulse is slowing," Cyril said before Quinton could reply.

Tavias released Quinton's shirt and they both turned to where Cyril crouched beside Kit, his fingers on her neck.

Quinton was at Kit's side in an instant, his hand flat on her bare chest, his magic trickling into her. Cyril was right. Kit's pulse was slower now. Too slow to maintain life. And that wasn't all. On the heels of the erratic rhythm of Kit's weakening heart, her lungs now struggled to draw air. Her body was failing her, each hardship tipping into the next like a string of falling dominos.

Collecting himself, Quinton poured his magic into Kit, taking control of her heart and lungs as he'd done on the Phoenix. Unlike then, when he'd slowed her breath and heart to calm her panic, now he spurred them into action. He made her heart beat, her lungs expand. Again and again and again.

Sweat trickled down Quinton's scales as he fought to keep Kit's body alive. It was like walking a tightrope – one misstep, and the consequences would be dire. He couldn't make a misstep. Couldn't let his attention wane for a moment. He had to keep her heart beating, because nothing else would.

"Quinton." Whoever said his name sounded far away and Quinton paid them no mind. He couldn't afford to. With every ounce of power that he pushed into Kit, the darkness seemed to pull her further away by just a hair's breadth more. It was like trying to hold onto sand that slipped through his fingers no matter how tightly he grasped it.

Kit's body spasmed, arching in Hauck's arms.

Not enough. Quinton wasn't doing enough for her. He had to do more.

"Quinton, you are going to burn out."

Gathering all of his life force, Quinton channeled it into his mate. The world blurred. The sounds dampened. None of it mattered though because Kit needed *more* and Quinton wasn't enough.

He wasn't enough. All his magic, all his training, none of it was enough to overpower the void that sought to claim his mate. The weight of this truth bore into him, cold and unyielding.

"Quinton!" Cyril shook him. "You have to stop."

"He won't," Hauck answered. He must have pulled Cyril off because Quinton no longer felt his brother's hands on his shoulder. "She is his mate. He is not going to let her go."

"He can't hold her anymore," Cyril said, the truth twisting the knife deeper in Quinton's soul.

"He can if he has help," Hauck said quietly.

Something about Hauck's words pierced through Quinton's haze. He snapped his head up in time to see Hauck bare his canines. In time to understand what his brother intended to do.

"Don't," Quinton ground out.

"She needs more than what you can offer," said Hauck. "But maybe not more than both of us can."

"It will bind your life, Hauck," Quinton gritted out, pain and anger wrestling within him as he fought a war on two fronts. His mate and his brother. "You mate her, and if she dies... if she dies, you die. Don't you understand that?"

"I do," Hauck responded softly, his gaze never wavering from Kit's face. "For once, I know exactly what I'm doing." With no further hesitation, Hauck struck, biting Kit's shoulder.

The moment Hauck's teeth pierced Kit's flesh, her body jolted, the bond between them igniting like a spark catching on dry tinder. Quinton gasped, the overwhelming force of the new connection surging through him. He clenched his jaw, fighting to keep control of his magic and Kit's heart as the power of Hauck's life force joined the battle for their mate.

Tavias and Cyril moved together, the twins not bothering with words. They struck with a dragon's primal drive, each staking their claim on Kit's flesh—and offering their life in return.

Quinton felt himself swept into the center of a storm, energies swirling around him, battering him from every side. With each additional bond, the weight on Quinton increased, but so did the hope. It was the five of them now, a pack in truth. Power ripped through their shared connection, each strand of magic, every fiber of love and determination, working in tandem to give Kit the strength she needed.

The energy circulating within Kit was palpable. Quinton could feel her there, fighting for herself. Fighting for the pack. And yet… and yet her body remained eerily still, with not a single flutter of an eyelash or twitch of a finger to indicate the consciousness Quinton knew was there.

In his peripheral vision, a glint of the brand on Kit's forearm caught Quinton's focus. Beneath the pair of overlapping circles, Kit's forearm was red and hot, the skin straining against something beneath it. Quinton didn't know whether his next motion was born of guttural instinct or sudden understanding. His hand moved, unsheathing his blade, its polished surface glinting in the stray beams of sunlight. With one swift cut, Quinton slid the blade across the Kit's brand, breaking the interlocking circles apart.

CHAPTER 26

Kit

I love the cabin. It's in the mountains, surrounded by tall whispering pines and has a crystal clear pond I can swim in anytime I want. My mother swims with me too, splashing and laughing and tossing me into the water. We've been here for two months—longer than we've stayed anywhere that I remember.

I'm sitting at the kitchen table, finishing up my supper as I swing my legs back and forth on the large chair. My toes just reach the oak floor and the sunlight streaming through a window casts dappled patterns everywhere. But it's the way the sunlight dances upon my mother's scales, those iridescent patterns on her temples, that captivates me. They glow, emitting hues of azure and lilac, playing with the light.

I want to touch her scales. She has them out so rarely because there are bad people who would hurt her for having them. I'm never ever allowed to have my scales out, not even when we are alone.

"Are there seconds?" I ask, finishing off strips of deer meat. They are delicious and fresh from the hunt.

"You may, but first, come here, Kit." My mother beckons me to her, her movements seamless and graceful, yet I can feel the air thickening with something heavy. "It's alright," she adds.

I don't believe her. Her luminescent beauty is a stark contrast with the sorrow in her eyes. Deep, sapphire pools filled with pain and determination. I walk to her tentatively and she pulls me to stand between her knees, her fingers brushing my hair.

"Kit," my mother's voice is a haunting melody that makes my stomach clench. Something is wrong. I know it is. She is going to tell me that we can't stay in this cabin anymore or go to the pond. Her smile is sad. "You are my star. You shine in the darkest of nights, the last hope of our lineage. The Order of Orion won't rest until they have you."

I'm confused. "But Mama, you're a dragon too," I blurt out, even though I know better than to say that word. "So I'm not the last. There are two of us."

She sighs softly, ruffling my hair. "Yes, sweetling. But your destiny eclipses mine. It's woven with ancient prophecies."

I shrug. I don't care much about prophecies. I care about

the pond. About why my mother looks so sad. "Don't be scared, Mama. The order can't find us here."

"They can find us anywhere," she tells me.

"But why would they look? We aren't doing anything."

"Female dragons are very special, Kit. Do you know what females can do that males can't?"

"Lay eggs, of course."

"That's right. The order wants to kill us because we can lay eggs. Without dames, the dragon race will not survive. That's what the order wants, what they've been working on for hundreds and hundreds and hundreds of years."

"So we have to hide," I say.

"So we have to hide." There is a note to my mother's voice that makes me worry that she is talking about something different than what we've always done. "You are getting bigger, sweetling. I won't be able to hide your scales soon."

"But you hide yours."

She sighs. "It's different."

"I don't understand."

"I know." She hugs me close, her scent of pine and earth, enveloping me in love and sorrow. "You have to hide, Kitterny. Have to hide so well that the order will never find you. Not until you grow and become stronger, and have a pack that will fly beside you. One day you will rise and spread your wings. But until then, you must be human."

Panic rushes through me. I don't understand what my mother is saying, but I know I don't like it.

"You have a journey ahead, Kit. It will be scary at times,

but it has to be thus. And then, when the moment is right, you will embrace who you truly are."

"How will I know?"

"Because one day, there will be a human girl. She will have hair white as snow, and will control the wind. Stay close to that girl, sweetling. She will be your key." My mother pulls out a box but doesn't open it. I can see two overlapping circles engraved on the top though. Then she takes out a vile from her pocket and tips a few drops of its liquid into my tea. "Drink your tea now."

"What will it do?"

"It will lock your essence, making you seem like any other human child," she says, but there are tears in her eyes. I think the tea will do more than she is saying. I know it will. "You have to drink it," she tells me. "You have to, Kit. There is no choice."

And so I do.

CHAPTER 27

Hauck

Quinton's incision cut Kit's brand clean in half, breaking the continuity of the interlocking circles. In the next heartbeat, a rush of iridescent magic exploded from the severed mark, swirling like a tempest around Kit. It was as if a dam had burst, releasing pent-up power that had been trapped. Suppressed. The room crackled with energy, the air shifting and vibrating. Or maybe it wasn't the air, maybe it was Hauck's lifeblood.

Hauck's arms tightened around Kit on instinct, though the heat radiating from the rushing magic seared his skin. She arched in his hold, flailing amidst the pack surrounding her as her citrus and cinnamon scent melded with a whiff of something primal and ancient and so powerful that it stole Hauck's breath.

The soft curves of Kit's ears elongated, the tips becoming more defined and pointed like the immortal fae. Her cheekbones shifted too, morphing from beautiful to ethereal as a fine row of iridescent scales emerged along her temples. They shimmered in the low light, reflecting a myriad of colors and wound their way down her neck and body. Kit's previously erratic pulse now thrummed with a steady, powerful rhythm that Hauck felt echoed inside him.

Lub-dub. Lub-dub. Lub-dub.

The beating of Kit's heart, and Hauck's own, of the whole pack's, sounded as one. And with that single joint pulse, the connection surging between them intensified. The bond howled with life and joy and so much power that Hauck both feared the camp would explode around them and didn't care if it did.

As the torrent of escaping magic settled and Kit's body relaxed back into Hauck's hold, her eyes finally fluttered open. Elongated chocolate-colored irises met Hauck's wide eyed gaze.

"Hello," Hauck whispered. He meant to sound quip, but what came out was pure reverence.

Hello dame, hello mate, hello queen, the dragon inside him purred, adding a very explicit visual suggesting exactly what to do with the perfect naked female splayed in his arms.

Racing to stay ahead of his sudden lust, Hauck set Kit

carefully on the bedroll and pulled off his shirt to wrap around her. "You are alive then, turnip. Welcome back."

Kit blinked, twisting around to look at the pack. Everyone's attention was on her now. Tavias, Cyril, and Quinton all staying preternaturally still as they tracked each of Kit's movements.

"I'm alive," Kit repeated Hauck's words back to him in a whisper. She looked haunted. Uncertain. She pushed herself up, testing her arms gingerly before putting weight on them. "I was sure I was going to die. The priests..." She shuddered.

Hauck's fingers curled into fists. The priests hurt his mate. They would pay.

"The priests changed the weather, we know," Cyril said. "You'd fallen in the snow and passed out from the cold."

"No." She shook her head. Colors danced along her scales. Hauck had never seen anything like it. "I didn't fall. The priests paralyzed me on purpose. They wanted me dead, but they needed it to appear natural. Gave me an orange potion that paralyzes humans. They said there was no antidote. They were wrong."

The priests would die. First though... Hauck cleared his throat. "I don't think they were wrong."

"Of course they were." She frowned. "I can move now, can't I? This is all real?"

Tavias and Cyril exchanged glances, but neither of the twins seemed inclined to join this particular conversation. Hauck knew better than to look to Quinton for something as difficult as words. "Oh, you are very real." Hauck assured her.

He shifted, trying to relieve the pressure on his cock, which likewise wanted for the talking to be done with. "And yes, you are moving just fine. That part you have right."

"What part do I have wrong?" asked Kit.

"The human part."

"What?"

Moving slowly, Hauck ran his thumb softly along the line of scales that now wound down Kit's temple. She jerked and the sudden gust of arousal filling her scent made Hauck chuckle.

Kit's scales shifted to purple.

Hauck laughed aloud, then winced. Kit's arousal had sent his already volatile lust sky rocketing. The fresh mating bond strained between them, demanding to be appeased. The others were shifting too, drawing closer to her now. The dragons inside them all couldn't bare the extra space.

"I'm not human?" Kit said, as if tasting the words.

"You aren't," Tavias confirmed. He reached forward and tucked a strand of hair behind Kit's pointed ear. Hauck wondered if Tavias was fighting the urge to trace his hand along the mating bite as badly as Hauck was.

"I'm not human," she repeated, sounding more certain now. Her eyes widened. "I'm... I never was human."

"Not really sure about the historical aspect," Hauck murmured. It was getting difficult to breath without touching Kit's skin. He picked up her hand and stroked his thumb along her skin. The contact soothed something in his soul even as it fueled his lust.

"I remember," Kit insisted, her intense gaze sweeping across them all. Cyril and Quinton crouched close, their attention on her. "The Order of Orion and my mother and... The mortal with white hair and air magic. The one I was supposed to find. Who was going to lead me back to me."

"I hope one of you lot understood any of that," Hauck muttered to his brothers. Kit's scales were *iridescent*. He'd never seen anything like them. "Maybe you can explain it all to me. Later. A lot later."

"Are you talking about the prophecy?" Tavias asked Kit. It was all Hauck could do not to punch him. "From distant lands, a mortal strays, with locks of white and air that plays. That part?"

Kit nodded.

Cyril picked up the stupid poem where Tavias left off. "Thus rises one that's strong and true, who'll conjure life her soul imbued."

"Her spirit fierce," Quinton said. Rutting Quinton. "- her power vast, her fate entwined with dragons' past."

Oh for star's sake. Hauck ran his fingers through Kit's hair, savoring its silky feel along his skin. "I hate to be the bearer of bad news, but she isn't actually blond, remember? This is dye."

"That's not the part that's about her," Quinton said, adding *you idiot* with his clipped tone.

"No," said Kit. "Cordelia. That first part of the prophecy, it was about Cordelia. I think—"

"You do as you wish," Hauck interrupted, "but I'm done

thinking." Closing the short distance between them, Hauck pressed his mouth to Kit's.

Kit let out a short gasp before opening herself to him, the mating bond between them roaring and vibrating with need. On his knees, Hauck tangled his fingers tightly in Kit's hair, anchoring them together as he savored her warmth and taste and soul. Kit tasted of citrus and power, of something new and ancient all rolled into one. She tasted gloriously of herself.

Alive. She was alive and she was his, and he was hers, and they were here. Everything else anyone wanted to talk about could go to rutting hell and wait its turn.

CHAPTER 28

Kit

I remember. I remember everything.

And right now, with Hauck's mouth on mine, I don't give one damn about any of it. My head tingles where Hauck has his hands tangled in my hair, the tiny prickles driving me as wild as the press of his tongue in my mouth. Need rushes through me, more potent than anything I've felt before.

I grip onto Hauck's shoulders, pressing deeper into the kiss. My body pushes toward him as if the torrent of magic that had just swept over me is hitting me again. More. More More. I need more. More than just kissing. And more than Hauck alone.

And it's not just me. There is a presence inside me, a

primal roaring presence that is both me and not me. And it wants too.

The potency of it is frightening.

Pulling my mouth off Hauck's, even for a moment, hurts. I pant as I scour the shelter to find Quinton in the pack, traces of panic spurring my heart into a faster beat. The control I have of my body, the one the pack has worked so hard for is slipping away into something different entirely.

Quinton's intense silver eyes soften. "It's alright, huma—" he winces, quickly correcting himself. "Kitterny. Let the frenzy take you. You don't need to stop it. There will be time to think later."

"You *really* don't need to stop it," Hauck adds, even though no one asked him. His face is strained. So are his flies.

Strong hands brush over my back and shoulders, and I realize that Tavias and Cyril have come up together, like the twins they are. Their breaths are warm against my skin and their scents fill my lungs. Familiar yet magnified. They smell male and dominant and powerful and needy and mine.

Their mouths close around my breasts, each suckling fiercely on the sensitive flesh. Their hands roam over me, the heat from their skin searing into mine. My hands are roaming their bodies right back and there is nothing gentle or tentative about my touch as I rake my fingers over their muscular forms, the roughness of their scars and the smoothness of their tattoos. The jolting edges of the scales.

My tongue runs the length of scales on Cyril's neck.

He roars and bites into me. The pain is sharp, exploding from my breast and blooming into molten pleasure.

I buck my hips, seeking more, more, more.

Hauck is there, shoving my thighs apart and bringing his mouth to my dripping sex. The first lick is so intense, so shocking, that I am left breathless. And then another. And then another, each one more intense than the last as Hauck adds the scrape of his canines to the assault of sensation he is launching at my core.

Cyril and Tavias shift their mouths to my neck, nipping and suckling as they run their hands possessively over my body. Their tongues are burning hot along my scales. Stars. The damn sensitive scales. How do they live with these?

Magic pours from me, slipping around the males' fingers, lashing at their skin.

I can't stop it.

Can't even slow the tendrils of power. Magic spills all around, pouring from all of the places the males touch.

I writhe.

Tavias grabs my wrists, pinning them above my head to the ground. Amethyst fire burns in his eyes and he snarls with uncontrolled lust.

I shove at him with my magic but meet a hard wall of silver that is so intimately familiar that I nearly find release from the collision alone. Though he still stands away from the pack, Quinton is vibrating with power that's now battling mine.

Hauck's hands tighten on the inside of my thighs and he

plunges inside me. Not his tongue now, but his cock, which is so much thicker and longer than it has a right to be.

He thrusts hard, like he is going to conquer me and I wrap my legs around his waist to pull him deeper still.

A beast-like roar fills the shelter, drowning out the storm outside. It takes a moment to realize that it is me. My voice. My roar.

My back arches and a keening cry breaks from my lips as I explode with power, breaking Tavias's grip and rolling Hauck until it's him on his back and me riding his shaft.

My mind splinters as the magic, the power and the curve of Hauck's cock inside me launches me into another dimension. My body explodes and I'm left screaming, writhing and begging for more.

And more is given.

As Hauck thrusts into me wildly, Tavias rocks me forward and takes me from the back. The double penetration magnified each stroke of their cocks. In and out, in and out. So hard and fierce that it should rip me to shreds, but it doesn't.

Because I'm no longer mortal.

The scales along their cocks are warm and harder-edged than I've ever felt before as they flare and shift inside me. They scrape and bite, lighting up every nerve inside me with pleasure so intense it's cruel.

Cyril's fingers tangle in my hair and he forces my head back. My mouth opens and he takes it, flooding me with his taste. The kiss is as possessive as the grip he has on my hair, whatever gentleness lives inside the dragon is gone in favor of the claiming.

I'm glad for it. My nails rake down his abs and along the column of scales on his belly. I can feel Cyril quiver at that and see the way his scales flare and shift color frantically.

My lips move to the scales on his neck, licking and biting and tasting him.

Cyril's grip on my hair tightens as my teeth break his skin. The taste of blood mingles with his taste of ocean and unlocks another visceral gate deep inside my core. Power floods from him into me, a force and a presence that is more than just him. It is everything that he is and the place where he came from and it all feels like a part of me now.

My power is pulsing, growing and spilling into the pack in a mix of thrusts and jolts of power and pleasure. I anchor myself against Cyril, taking the males as deeply as I can.

But even with riding Hauck's shaft, and Tavias's thrusting and the scrape of Cyril's teeth along my ear, it's not enough. I'm not whole.

"Quinton." I rasp the male's name and he inhales sharply. He still stands away, the lone dragon. The assassin. The shadow. The one who does not believe himself worthy of the pack, though his magic and mine are already intertwined. "Quinton," I say again, reaching out for his hand. "I need you. We all do."

"You don't," he says. "You are better without—"

"Quinton!" I howl his name as Hauck's cock strokes the deepest part of me and my channel contracts, clenching around his shaft. Pressure grows inside my body, seeking release that I refuse to accept without my whole pack here.

The storm outside our shelter is ferocious now. The wind is screaming as thunder and hail join the winter flurry. It pounds against the roof like wild drums, faster and harder and demanding.

Hauck and Tavias both thrust harder, pumping into me like they are going to die if they don't. I ride Hauck's cock while Tavias thrusts into my ass, his powerful hands holding me as my body shakes and spasms at the edge of pleasure.

And still, Quinton won't move.

"Please," I beg him.

That one word and he is beside me at once, Cryil shifting to give him space. Quinton's eyes glow with silver flame as he wraps his hand around my neck.

My eyes widen, my senses roaring at the threat that feels a thousand times more potent now that my dragon has awoken. But instead of fighting back, I lift my chin, giving my mate all the access he wants. Giving him my trust.

Quinton squeezes his grip, but the jolt of terror it brings morphs to a pleasure that magnifies everything. The rush of need in my channel, the screaming in the bundle of nerves that Cyril's fingers have now found, the rise of pleasure that is so dizzying that it's agony.

In my daze, I free Quinton's cock and take its velvety hardness into my mouth. I suck hard and Quinton throws his head back with a roar.

Yes. I like that roar. My dragon likes that roar too.

As I suck him, Quinton's power pours through our bond. I feel his heart as it beats, his soul as it burns and the magic that he is.

I feel it all and I know he feels me. I think the whole pack does.

The new surge of power is like a spur, and I ride Hauck and Tavias with an intensity that would have left me shaking before. But I'm not shaking now. I'm glowing. I'm radiating with magic that is purer, richer, and far more vibrant than before.

I can see it in the way the other males' scales shimmer and even in the way Quinton's eyes glow like silver flames.

I'm not the only one glowing.

"She is ready," Cyril says, his hand cupping my chin and tilting my head up to look into his eyes. They are filled with power, his pupils stretched to slits.

Hauck's brows draw down. His eyes are awash with the raging magic that is in me now.

The males are driving me to the point of madness. Their voices, their hands, their cocks, and my mouth, and their mouths, and their magic, and my magic. I need it all. Want it all.

Quinton leans down and brushes his lips along the sensitive scales along my temples. The gentleness is so at odds with everything that it sends me over the edge.

My climax feels like a blinding explosion of lights and power that is more than just a release. It's a claim. Iridescent power surrounds us, then explodes with a force that shatters the shelter into splinters of wood and vines. Hauck and Tavias come inside me, with magic as much as essence. Quinton's flavor explodes on my tongue, and moves into my body like the caress of a wave, Cyril's release doing the same along my skin.

I've never felt this way.

Powerful. Complete. Primal.

But now that I've had it, it'll never be enough.

I need this every day.

I need it all the time.

Now.

I need more.

And so we do it again and again, oblivious of the snow and hail and the raging storm.

CHAPTER 29

Kit

$\mathcal{T}$he final climax rakes over my body then subsides, the wave of exhaustion washing over me for the dozenth time. But it's different this time. I feel the fevered vice of the mating frenzy releasing its grip, and the reality—the memories—finding their way back into my consciousness. Between the bouts of soul consuming rutting, I managed to fill the males in on what I've learned about the Order of Orion and the memories my mother had sealed inside me. But I'd not had to face those words, not with the frenzy's pull pounding my instincts.

But now that escape is slipping away, and I'm terrified.

I struggle to catch my breath, the cold air stinging my lungs. The storm continues its relentless assault, and there is little left of the shelter to provide much protection from the elements now. A wall and a half. A part of the flooring. A lot of scattered branches.

"Hello there, nymph." Cyril runs a knuckle along my cheek and I feel the touch both in my skin and through the still raw mating bond connecting us. His blue eyes watch me intensely, concern spilling from beneath thick lashes. He too knows the reprieve of the frenzy is over.

My body aches, and I'm distantly aware of the bruises, scrapes, and bite marks that notch my skin. I chew my lip. Only I have elongated sharp canines now and instead of soothing myself I draw blood and yip.

Hauck coughs violently. Trying to cover up a laugh.

Cyril, the one closest to me right now, pulls me against him and covers me with a warm cloak. His breath is ragged and his body as slick with sweat as mine.

"We need to get out of the elements," Tavias says but I can tell he is being diplomatic. He wants to get me out of the elements. All four of them are watching my every breath and blink, as they had since the mating bond took hold. Quinton is already pulling on his clothes and weapons to take up guard and Tavias is getting a fire going. "You could help with the shelter you know," he tells Hauck. "Dealing with trees is your lane."

Hauck, who is laying flat on his back trying to catch falling hail in his mouth, makes a sound with the back of his throat. "I could... But I am quite content to be right where I am."

Tavias curses at him, the words rolling off like water from a duck. For a moment, everything seems normal again. Quinton brooding on guard, and Hauck driving Tavias mad while Cyril quietly surveys everything, plans already forming behind his intelligent gaze.

"I can help rebuild," I offer, pulling my cloak tight around me as I stand and stretch my hand toward the low hanging branches of the nearest tree. I'm not sure how I intend to weave the branches together, but there is power inside me now and it's itching to get out.

"Don't," all four males say at once.

"Why—" The branch explodes, shards of bark and pine raining down on our heads.

Tavias clears his throat and I remember what he'd once told me about not being permitted in haylofts while he was growing into his affinity for flame. Just then, a clump of snow drops onto my head and slides down the scales along my temple. The sensation is so intense I jump off the ground and Cyril grabs me before I stumble into the fire.

"I think I'm suddenly in the mood to do work," Hauck says, jumping to his feet with feline grace. He pulls on his britches and saunters off to join Tavias.

All isn't normal. Not at all. I'm a dragon. A dame. A creature that the Order of Orion had hunted into extinction to slowly kill off the dragons. I'm supposed to be the hope that Cordelia's life and death had ushered into being. The one that's supposed to change everything. Except I can't even manage the basics of keeping myself alive.

I know I should hold my head up and grab the torch of my destiny like a flag for all dragonkind. That's what my mother gave her life for. What everyone awaits. And instead, all I can think about is how much of a mistake the fates have made.

With only her shall dragons find, a future thriving and entwined, I recite the final lines of the prophecy in my mind. It says that the dragons can't have a thriving future without me. It doesn't say that with me they'll actually succeed.

Pulling away from Cyril, I finish getting dressed and help out with rebuilding the old fashioned way. Not that I'm much use. My body doesn't move the way it did before. With my changed strength, I misjudge half the wood I place onto the encampment and make the roof cave twice before Hauck suggests I aid in some other way. Except when I walk toward the fire, Tavias blocks my path outright.

Cyril catches a rabbit. It looks so enticing to the new primal dragon inside me, that I can't help snatching it out of his hands—only to get a mouthful of fur when I realize that despite my new instincts I've no idea how to eat a raw catch. Stars. Not only am I useless, but I'm a greater liability than I ever was as a human.

"I'm sorry," I tell Cyril as he leads me away from yet another near averted disaster and into the newly re-erected shelter. Hauck and the others put extra effort into reinforcing the shack, and it's even more spacious and comfortable than the original. There is even a cleverly arranged place for a small fire, laid out in a way as to keep the wooden walls and roof from going up in flames. Provided I don't do something stupid.

Cyril sits against the wall and pulls me against his muscled chest. His hand covers mine the way it has so many times before. I remember how his hand has always felt. Warm and rough and strong, providing a feeling of security that soothed me. Now I feel the whole tapestry of the peaks and valleys in his palm, the hard won calluses and tiny soft spots, the weight of history each mark carries. I feel the energy that flows between us. And I don't know what to do with any of it.

"Magic takes time to control," Cyril says. "We had decades to grow into our bodies and our power. You've had hours. Let's set our expectations a little more realistically."

Tavias tosses Cyril another cloak, which Cyril wraps around me, even though I tell them that I'm not cold. I think the males are all terrified of me freezing again and are not taking my word on anything that has to do with my new body. I can't exactly blame them, but still.

In the mountains beyond, a howling wind rips through the trees, accompanied by the distant sound of falling clumps of snow. But it isn't just a howling now. It's a symphony of varying wind currents, shifting branches and the subtle groans of the mountain itself. Suddenly I'm out there again, cold and paralyzed. Unable to even move my mouth away from the suffocating snow, or blink away specs of debris.

I don't realize I'm shaking until Cyril and Tavias and Hauck are all crowded around me, soothing me with their touch and voices. Quinton doesn't leave his station from outside guard duty, but I can feel his worry pulsating through the bond. A bond that I now realize I forced on them. They mated me because it was the only way to keep me alive. To keep Quinton alive. And now they are stuck with me.

"What was that thought?" Hauck asks suspiciously, his green eyes narrowing on me. He catches my chin before I can lower my face. "Tell me."

I shake my head.

"You know I have my ways of getting to the truth." He wags his brows, then blows along my scales. A shiver of electricity darts from each scale to the very base of my spine and lower, as if each tiny place is a receptor to a hidden world of sensation. My thighs tighten and rutting need surges through me, almost too intensely to control. Intensely enough to ache. Hauck gives me a knowing grin. "Ask me how long I can keep that up."

I shut my eyes, drawing deep breaths to get my damn body back under control. "Can you just stop," I growl with more force than I intended. Now that I've started though, the emotions spill from me. "All of you. Can you just stop pretending?"

I can feel them shifting. Exchanging glances. "Which part do you imagine is pretend?" Cyril clarifies carefully.

My eyes snap open. "The part where you pretend you are alright with this. With any of this." I wave my hands at myself. "You bound your lifeforce to me to save my life. But we all know you shouldn't have. I'm not—"

"I bound my lifeforce to you because I love you," Cyril says, interrupting me harshly.

"You? What?"

"I love you." This from Hauck.

"I love you." Tavias.

A jolt of heat through my mating bond with Quinton. My breath catches.

"We love you, nymph," Cyril says again, his voice having that note of confidence and command that I first saw on the Phoenix. The kind of voice that leaves no room for doubt. He brushes his thumb along my lip. "Stars, don't you understand that by now?"

"But what if I'm…" it hurts to say it aloud, but I do. "What if I'm not strong enough to be the dragon Massa'eve needs?"

"Our feelings have nothing to do with you being a human, or dragon, or a thread woven into some bloody prophecy," Tavias says. Sparks dance along his scales as if just the thought of that makes him furious. "It has everything to do with who you are. Who you make us be, when you are near."

Tavias kisses my forehead and Hauck toys with my wrist. Their touch is healing. Warm. More than I deserve.

"Speaking of our new mate," Hauck says, his attention on my shifting scales. "Since she is actually a dragon dame, she should be able to leave the trial ground's wards. So maybe we should be getting the hell out of here."

Out of the trial grounds. Away from the priests. It sounds divine.

"What about the priests? And the eggs I found?" I ask. "We can't just leave everything. And if we go past the wards, we can't come back. We have to do something now, while we are here."

"Can I remind you that literally everyone and everything here is designed to kill you, turnip? The other competitors, the priests, hell—even the weather." Hauck winces. "I'm not the military mastermind here, but you getting dead doesn't seem like a step in the right direction toward freedom of dragonkind."

"We have to expose the priests," I say. "And for that we need proof, not just some allegations or my memories. If we leave, Salazar and Geoffrey will make it known that we forfeited the trials and use that to spark the very civil war we came here to try and avoid."

"Kitterny is right," Tavias says. Hauck looks like he is ready to punch the dragon general, but Tavias shakes his head grimly. "Leaving here won't erase the target from her back. Our best chance to expose the order is from their stronghold."

"She is a bleeding dragon dame." Hauck throws his arms up. "The truth—"

"The truth won't matter," Cyril says grimly, his arms still around me. "Perception will. We won't have Massa'eve's attention long enough to even prove that Kitterny is a dragon. She was a child when she was bound. It will be decades before she has enough control and power to shift. Frankly, a tale that we've glued some scales onto a human in a desperate attempt to hide our shame at losing the trials is more believable than a tale claiming the revered priests are actually on a mission to exterminate dragonkind. We need proof. And we need to show it to a crowd."

"Like the one that will gather to see who's survived the second trial," I say.

Tavias nods. "For now, the priests have every reason to think they've won. We use that. And we use the week to gather evidence and discover just how deep the order's claws go. So long as no one knows that Kit is still alive, much less a dragon, we have the upper hand."

"Someone is coming." Quinton hollers from beyond the shelter. "A pack."

Within a heartbeat, the males have their swords but before they can even exit the shelter, a dragon crashes through our roof. And that quickly, our upper hand advantage is gone.

THANK YOU FOR READING DRAGONS' Mate. The adventures concludes in Dragons' Future, Her Royal Dragon Pack book 4. Get it now.

OTHER BOOKS BY THIS AUTHOR:

BOOKS IN THE WORLD OF LUNOS

POWER OF FIVE

Reverse Harem Romance

1. POWER OF FIVE

2. MISTAKE OF MAGIC

3. TRIAL OF THREE

4. LERA OF LUNOS

5. VEIL OF MEMORY

6. ROGUE OF GREAT FALLS ROGUE

7. BELL OF TRUTH

HER ROYAL DRAGON PACK

Reverse Harem Romance

1. DRAGONS' CAPTIVE

2. DRAGONS' BRIDE

3. DRAGONS' MATE

4. DRAGONS' FUTURE

IMMORTALS OF TALONSWOOD

Reverse Harem Romance

1. LAST CHANCE ACADEMY

2. LAST CHANCE REFORM

3. LAST CHANCE WITCH

4. LAST CHANCE WORLD*

Contains Power of Five cross-over. Can be considered Power o Five book 8.

* * *

TRIDENT RESCUE (Writing as A.L. Lidell)

Contemporary Enemies-to-Lovers Romance

ENEMY ZONE

ENEMY CONTACT

ENEMY LINES

ENEMY HOLD

ENEMY CHASE

ENEMY STAND

* * *

ABOUT THE AUTHOR

Alex Lidell is the Amazon Breakout Novel Awards finalist author of THE CADET OF TILDOR (Penguin) and several Amazon Top 100 Kindle Bestsellers, including the POWER OF FIVE romance series. She is an avid horseback rider who believes in eating dessert first. She writes as both Alex Lidell and A.L. Lidell.

Join Alex's newsletter for news, bonus content and sneak peeks: https://links.alexlidell.com/News

Find out more on Alex's website: www.alexlidell.com

SIGN UP FOR NEWS AND RELEASE NOTIFICATIONS

Connect with Alex!
www.alexlidell.com
alex@alexlidell.com

Made in the USA
Las Vegas, NV
20 June 2024

91265110R00156